Never had Carolyn seen Beau look as appealing as he did at this moment...

with a child cuddled against his bare chest and the soft light of love shining from his eyes.

All of this would be so much easier if he'd truly been the Neanderthal man she'd expected him to be. If he'd been a beer-guzzling, belly-scratching lowlife, she would have suffered no compunction about using any means necessary to take the twins away from him. But it was going to be difficult to take the boys away from this man....

Dear Reader,

Spring is on the way—and love is blooming in Silhouette Romance this month. To keep his little girl, FABULOUS FATHER Jace McCall needs a pretend bride—fast. Luckily he "proposes" to a woman who doesn't have to pretend to love him in Sandra Steffen's *A Father For Always*.

Favorite author Annette Broadrick continues her bestselling DAUGHTERS OF TEXAS miniseries with *Instant Mommy*, this month's BUNDLES OF JOY selection. Widowed dad Deke Crandall was an expert at raising cattle, but a greenhorn at raising his baby daughter. So when he asked Mollie O'Brien for her help, the marriage-shy rancher had no idea he'd soon be asking for her hand!

In *Wanted: Wife* by Stella Bagwell, handsome Lucas Lowrimore is all set to say "I do," but his number one candidate for a bride has very cold feet. Can he convince reluctant Jenny Prescott to walk those cold feet down the aisle?

Carla Cassidy starts off her new miniseries THE BAKER BROOD with *Deputy Daddy*. Carolyn Baker has to save her infant godchildren from their bachelor guardian, Beau Randolph. After all, what could he know about babies? But then she experienced some of his tender loving care....

And don't miss our other two wonderful books— *Almost Married* by Carol Grace and *The Groom Wore Blue Suede Shoes* by debut author Jessica Travis.

Happy Reading!

Melissa Senate,
Senior Editor

Please address questions and book requests to:
Silhouette Reader Service
U.S.: 3010 Walden Ave., P.O. Box 1325, Buffalo, NY 14269
Canadian: P.O. Box 609, Fort Erie, Ont. L2A 5X3

DEPUTY DADDY

Carla Cassidy

Silhouette
R O M A N C E™
Published by Silhouette Books
America's Publisher of Contemporary Romance

SILHOUETTE BOOKS

ISBN 0-373-19141-3

DEPUTY DADDY

Books by Carla Cassidy

CARLA CASSIDY

is the author of young-adult novels, as well as many contemporary romances. She's been a cheerleader for the Kansas City Chiefs football team and has traveled the East Coast as a singer and dancer in a band, but the greatest pleasure she's had is in creating romance and happiness for readers.

LONG ISLAND BUSINESSMAN MURDERED

(Long Island)—Joseph Baker, president of Baker Enterprises, was found dead in his office on Friday night. Although police are looking into motives, a suspect was seen fleeing from the scene of the crime. The police are looking for Sam Baker, the son of the murdered man, in connection with the crime. Anyone with any information as to Mr. Baker's whereabouts is urged to contact their local law enforcement agency.

Chapter One

Carolyn Baker frowned as she turned the rental car off Main Street and onto Elm. Fumbling in her purse, she withdrew the letter that contained the address of Beau Randolf.

It shouldn't be too hard to find his house. Casey's Corners, Kansas, was the smallest town she'd ever been in. "No way," she said aloud. There was positively no way she would allow her godchildren to be raised in this godforsaken blink-of-an-eye town that didn't even warrant an official spot on a map.

She slowed the car to a crawl, scanning the numbers on the houses she passed. Reluctantly she noted that the homes were neat, the yards well kept. It was a pleasant enough neighborhood, but that didn't mean it was the right place for her godsons to be brought up.

When she spotted Beau's address she pulled to a halt in front. Shutting off the engine, she sat for a moment and simply looked at the house.

It wasn't too bad—a two-story with a wraparound front porch. Spring flowers blossomed in the sunshine, dancing their colors along the walk. The early-morning light was kind, casting golden hues across the front of the house. Still, unlike the other houses she'd passed, this place cried out for a new coat of white paint, and the lawn desperately needed tending.

No way, she repeated to herself. She simply couldn't allow it. Mary's twins deserved better than this small town and their countrified godfather, Beau Randolf. Her heart clutched with grief as she thought of Bob and Mary. It was so hard to believe that they were really gone, killed in an automobile accident a month ago. That made four people in the past few months who had been ripped unexpectedly, unreasonably, away from her. One month ago her father had been murdered and her brother had disappeared.

Sam, where are you? Thoughts of her older brother, who had vanished from his wife and child, vanished seemingly from the face of the earth, caused her to grip the steering wheel tightly. Hopefully she would find some answers to Sam's disappearance while she was here. Before the tragedy of the car accident three weeks ago, Mary had called Carolyn and told her she thought she'd seen Sam in Casey's Corners. At that time Carolyn had done nothing about it. Since Sam's disappearance, sightings of him had been as commonplace as sightings of Elvis. He'd been spotted in nearly every state.

Before she sank completely into maudlin thoughts and unanswered questions, she got out of the car. Now was not the time to think of Sam. Carolyn had to settle the question of the custody of Mary's children before she could fully delve into the mystery of her father's murder and her older brother's disappearance.

She tried to smooth out the wrinkles in her beige suit. For as much as she'd paid for it, she had expected it to travel better than it had. She gave the skirt a final pat, then walked up the sidewalk toward the house.

As she stepped up onto the porch, she was greeted by the sound of screaming. The piercing wails radiated out from someplace in the back of the house. She knocked on the screen door, the knock immediately swallowed by more cries.

"Hello?" she called out, rapping more loudly on the door. She hesitated a moment, then opened the door and stepped into a living room that looked as if it had been hit by a baby tornado. A playpen filled with toys sat in the middle of the floor. A pile of clothes covered one side of the sofa and a stack of folded clothing hid the top of the end table. "Hello...?" She stumbled over a plastic rattle and stepped right on the smiling face of a rag doll. The whole place was a wreck. "Hello? Is anyone here?" she yelled again, afraid to advance any farther without permission.

The crying of the babies came closer and suddenly a man stepped into the doorway, in front of where Carolyn stood. He was big. He filled the space with his height and width. His dark hair stood on end, as if fingers of frustration had raked through it a dozen times. His eyes gleamed a wicked shade of gray and his mouth was compressed into a tight line of frustration. He was clad in blue jeans and babies. Carolyn realized that most of his bulk came from the two boys riding on his hips, who were both red-faced and screaming.

"Thank God you're here," the man said without preamble. "Come on in." Without waiting for her reply, he turned and disappeared back into the room from which he'd come.

Carolyn frowned. He acted like he'd been expecting her, but that was impossible. Nobody except her two sisters knew her plans. Curious, she followed him into a large, spacious kitchen where chaos seemed to be the prevailing decorative style. Dirty dishes towered precariously in the sink, and the countertops were somewhere beneath a collection of baby bottles, diapers and toys.

"Here . . . if you feed this one, I'll change the other one."

Carolyn tried to sputter a protest as he thrust one of the identical boys into her arms, but the child's vocal cords worked better than hers, effectively drowning her out. "Just use either high chair," he continued. "Their breakfast is on the plates in the microwave." He grabbed a disposable diaper from the stack in the center of the kitchen table. "I'm so glad the agency sent you over so quickly. I wasn't expecting anyone until later this morning." He flashed her a quick smile. "I'll be back in a second."

Carolyn stared after him for a moment, then looked down at the squealing child in her arms. She couldn't tell if he looked like either of his parents. At the moment he looked like a creature from another planet. His face was blotchy with splashes of red, his eyes were tightly closed and the sound emanating from his mouth proclaimed the healthy condition of his lungs. She didn't even know which one she held, Trent or Brent.

"Shh, there, there," she said, the dull throb of a headache beginning in the back of her neck. She'd only seen the babies once, when Mary and Bob had brought them to New York six months ago. At that time the babies had been four months old, nearly bald and wrapped in sweet-smelling blankets. She wrinkled her nose. This one didn't have that sweet baby scent she remembered. He smelled . . . sour.

Wrestling him into one of the high chairs, she then hurried to the microwave. She quickly punched the timer for a minute, unable to believe that such an enormous noise could come from such a small body.

She sighed in relief as the timer rang. She grabbed one of the Mickey Mouse plates inside. "Okay, okay. It's coming," she told the impatient diner. She pulled a chair up in front of the high chair and stared at the plate of food. Gross. Did kids really eat this stuff? There was a glob of white, a glob of yellow and a glob of orange, all with the consistency of apple sauce. Still, despite the disgusting conglomeration, the sight of the plate changed the little boy's screams to hiccuping jerks.

Carolyn took the baby spoon and put a little bit of the white stuff into his mouth, watching in fascination as he swallowed some, then spit a little bit back out. The last of his tears dried as he banged his fists against the top of the tray, obviously anxious for the next bite.

As Carolyn shoveled in one bite after another, she thought of the man in the next room. Her eyes narrowed in distaste. Beau Randolf. She'd never met the man before, but she'd heard enough about him to know she couldn't stand him. He hadn't even had the decency to let her know about Mary and Bob's funeral until it was too late for her to attend . . . and now he wanted custody of their children.

He'd apparently been expecting somebody . . . somebody from an agency. Somebody hired to help with the kids? Hmm. Her mind whirled with suppositions.

The sound of crying still came from wherever he had disappeared to and the sound filled her with a smug sense of satisfaction. He was obviously in way over his head. It was better she took custody immediately than let him father the kids for a couple of weeks or months, then bail out.

She refocused her attention on the little boy in front of her. She guided the last spoonful of the orange goop into his mouth, eminently pleased with herself. He'd cleaned the plate lickety-split and he wasn't crying anymore. Thank God. On the flight from New York, then later on the hour-long drive to Casey's Corners, she'd had momentary doubts about raising twin ten-month-old boys. But she could handle it.

After all, women were naturally maternal, weren't they?

"There, isn't that better?" she said, then frowned. He had an odd look on his little face and a strange rumbling noise came from his tummy. "What's the matter, baby? Did I feed you too fast?"

She leaned forward to wipe his mouth and at that moment, Carolyn learned firsthand the meaning of "projectile."

Moments later, when Beau returned to the kitchen, she was standing at the sink. She turned around and his gaze immediately focused on the huge orange stain that decorated the breast of her suit jacket. Irritation swept through her at the smile of amusement that danced on his lips for a moment, then disappeared.

"Oh, I forgot to tell you, Brent really hates apricots. The plate without the apricots was for him."

"Thanks for the warning," she said sharply as she gave her jacket a final dab with a wet sponge.

"He's got deadly accuracy when he spits."

"He didn't spit. He fired a missile." She placed the sponge back in the sink. "I've never seen anything like it before." She wanted to ask him if this sort of thing was normal, but instead opted to bite the inside of her cheek. She didn't want him thinking she knew nothing about babies. "How do you tell them apart?"

"Socks. Brent wears blue and Trent wears white." She watched as he put Trent in the second high chair and grabbed the remaining plate from the microwave. "Why don't you sit down and we'll discuss the job while I feed Trent." She hesitated a moment, then sat.

"I don't know how much the people at the agency told you about the position, but here's the deal. These boys are the sons of one of my best friends." His gray eyes darkened. "He and his wife were killed in a car accident a couple of weeks ago. I've petitioned the court for custody of them and should get a ruling in a few weeks. I'm going to raise these boys as my own."

"That's a pretty big task for a single man," she observed, talking loud enough to be heard over Brent's fist-banging on his plate.

"That's why I called the agency. I need somebody who can keep the house organized and watch the kids while I'm at work." His strong jaw knotted with determination. "Yes, it's a big task, but if I don't take them they'll be swallowed up by social services." He frowned. "Or, God forbid, turned over to the dragon woman."

"The dragon woman?"

"The wicked godmother. You know, like in the fairy tale, the one who gives Rapunzel the poisoned apple?" He spooned some white stuff into Trent's mouth, efficiently catching what bounced back out onto the spoon.

"It was a wicked stepmother." Carolyn swallowed hard against her anger. The dragon woman, indeed. He couldn't even keep his fairy tales straight.

"Pardon me?" He reached over and took the plate away from the future little drummer.

"In the fairy tale, it was a wicked stepmother, and it wasn't Rapunzel, it was Snow White."

"Whatever. I'm really not up on my bedtime stories." He redirected his attention to Trent. "Did the agency mention that this would be a live-in position?''

"Actually, they were rather vague about the particulars. They just said you were most anxious for help.''
Carolyn suddenly realized fate had put her in a perfect position. As the godfather, Beau wanted custody of Bob and Mary's twins. As the godmother, she wanted the same. How better to gain evidence of Beau Randolf's utter incapability than by living here and observing him for a week or two. She shoved the fact that it was slightly dishonest out of her head. After all, she had a mission—a mission born of love for Mary and the sweet little boys she'd left behind.

"Desperate is more like it.'' He spooned the last of the food into Brent's mouth. "They've only been here for less than a week, and as you can see, things have gone from clutter to chaos.''

She frowned. "But you said their parents died a couple of weeks ago. Why have they only been here a week?'' She already knew the answer, but was aware that if she was going to play the part of a complete stranger, she'd better play it for all she had. In for a penny... in for a pound.

"Right after the accident, Bob's mother, Iris, took the kids. She's a fine woman, and as their only family member, we thought it was for the best. Unfortunately, she had a mild stroke a week ago and realized she couldn't handle the strain at her age. So, here they are.''

Carolyn nodded. Immediately after she'd found out about the accident, she'd checked on the children and discovered they were with Bob's mother. She had thought it best they be with family. But Beau was no more family than she was. "Who has been watching them in the past week while you've been at work?"

"I took a leave of absence until I could get things arranged, but now that you're here, I'll get down to the station immediately...as soon as I can get dressed."

It was at that instant that Carolyn realized for the first time that Beau was bare-chested. In all the commotion of feeding the twins, she hadn't noticed. Now she couldn't imagine how she could have missed it. It was such a big chest, so broad with muscles and with just enough springy dark hair to make it interesting.

She averted her gaze in time to spy Brent reaching for a knife that had been carelessly left on the countertop. She grabbed the sharp instrument and moved it out of his grasp, mentally starting a list of reasons why Beau Randolf wasn't qualified to be the sole parent of these babies.

He stood and grinned at her. She supposed he thought the smile was charming, but it did nothing to endear him to her. Nothing he would do could accomplish that.

"This is crazy," he said, "but the agency didn't tell me your name and with all the commotion when you arrived, I forgot to ask."

"Caro-Carol. Carol Cook." It wasn't a lie; not exactly. Carolyn Baker, Carol Cook...close enough.

"Well, it's great having you here, Carol. Now I'll just get dressed and get out of your hair."

"Wait!" She stopped him before he headed out of the kitchen. "Uh...don't you want to show me around the house, let me know where things are?"

"The twins' things are in the bedroom with the cribs. Your room is the one with the single bed. At the moment the rest of the house is so disorganized it wouldn't do me any good to tell you where things are supposed to be. Feel free to reorganize anything you want to. If you'll give me your keys I'll bring your bags in from the car."

"They're in the back seat and the car isn't locked," she answered, mentally battling with her conscience over her role in this case of mistaken identity.

A few minutes later he stuck his head back into the kitchen. "Your suitcases are just inside the front door. I should be home by five or five-thirty this evening." He flashed her that same sexy, obnoxious smile. "It will be great to come home to a clean house and a hot meal. See you this evening, darlin'."

Carolyn's mouth opened and closed indignantly, but he was gone before she could come up with a proper retort to his casual endearment. "Darlin', indeed," she scoffed. She rose from her chair and eyed the kitchen distastefully. She knew Beau Randolf's type. A beer-swilling redneck who loved his gun collection and twangy, nasal music. The only place a woman would have in his life would be in the kitchen cleaning and cooking, and in his bed moaning about his prowess. Mary had told Carolyn about his penchant for dating a string of women, usually ones with lots of curves and no brains.

She sank back down at the table, her thoughts scattered. Thank God she had received the letter yesterday from the court announcing Beau's petition for custody. The dirty rat hadn't even had the guts to inform her himself.

All she had to do was get enough incriminating evidence on Beau to sway the judge to rule in her favor. If worse came to worst, she had enough money so she could tie the case up in court forever. She smiled at the thought. She would keep it in litigation until he was so broke the judge would give her custody because he had no place to live but a tent. Her smile slowly faded. She didn't want to go that route. Hurting Beau wasn't something she wanted to do—but she would do whatever was necessary to effect what was best for the twins. And it was best that they lived with her.

"Well, time is wasting," she said aloud. If she was going to play this role properly, she was going to have to whip this place into shape. It was a monumental task, but she was bright, she was energetic, and most of all she was motivated.

She looked at the twins. Both stared at her with huge blue eyes. A ripple of apprehension crawled up her spine. She had the distinct feeling that they both knew she was a fraud. At that moment their faces screwed up and they wailed.

Chapter Two

Beau whistled tunelessly as he drove down Main Street. He'd hardly been out of the house since taking over the care of the twins and it felt good to be out in the fresh air and morning sunshine.

Thank God the agency had come through so quickly with help. He'd only talked to them the day before, finally admitting to himself that caring for two infants was going to require more than just a part-time baby-sitter during the hours he worked. For the past week, while he'd learned the twins' routine, chaos had taken over.

Beau was determined to do right by those kids. He hadn't had any siblings of his own and Bob had been like a brother to him. Beau shoved away the pain of bereavement as he thought of his friend. Two years ago Beau had convinced Bob and Mary to leave New

York behind and move back here, to Casey's Corners. Beau had been a frequent visitor to their home. He'd been thrilled when they had asked him to be godfather to the twins, and he was determined to raise the boys the way he knew Bob would have wanted them raised.

Surely things would settle down, now that Carol Cook had arrived. Women had a natural touch when it came to caring for kids and organizing a home. In no time at all she would have the house whipped into shape and everything running smoothly.

He pulled up in front of the police station. It would be good to be back at work. Even though being a deputy sheriff in Casey's Corners, Kansas, couldn't compare with work on a force in a larger town, Beau was proud of his position, proud of his hometown. Unlike Bob, Beau had never had the desire to leave, to see what other parts of the country had to offer. Beau knew that Casey's Corners was his little piece of heaven. After a while, even Bob had admitted how much he'd missed the tiny town and was glad he'd brought his new wife back here to live.

"Hey, boss." Waylon Walker hurriedly pulled his feet off Beau's desk as Beau entered the small office. The chubby deputy stood, hauling his britches up over his generous bulk. "Wasn't expecting you in until tomorrow."

"That agency your wife suggested I call came through. My new housekeeper showed up a little while ago at the house." Beau motioned Waylon back down in the chair.

"Let me guess.... Fifties, with a gray bun and hips a man could get lost in?" Waylon picked at his teeth with an unbent paper clip.

Beau laughed and shook his head. "That's pretty much what I expected. Try late twenties or so, long dark brown hair and hips that would look great in a tight pair of jeans."

"You're kidding, right?" Waylon tossed the clip into the garbage.

Beau shook his head again. "No joke."

"Damn, it's not fair. Last summer Regina hired a woman to help with the kids while she had her hysterectomy, and I swear, she was nothing even remotely attractive. The woman had a mustache and muscles bigger than mine, for crying out loud."

Beau laughed. In truth, that was more like what he'd expected. He certainly hadn't expected someone like Carol Cook. Although she had been cool and rather uptight, she'd definitely been a looker—a looker with a cute butt. He shoved this thought out of his head.

"Single or married?" Waylon asked, a sly twinkle in his eyes.

"Single. Since it's a live-in arrangement, the agency said she would be single, but don't get any ideas. This arrangement has to stay strictly platonic." The last thing Beau needed was a physical attraction to his new housemate. There was too much at risk. It was best to keep things on a business level only. He wasn't particularly interested in a long-term relationship, and there was no reason to take chances with his new help. He didn't want the woman getting mad and walking off.

He needed things to work out so a judge would see that he was eminently qualified to care for the boys.

He needed Carol Cook's expertise in homemaking and child care far more than he needed any romantic entanglement. He had to make certain the wealthy barracuda from Manhattan had no grounds for getting custody of the boys away from him. "I can't afford to screw this up and let the godmother get those kids," Beau said after a moment.

"What's so bad about this godmother? Every time you mention her, you get a sneer on your face," Waylon observed.

Beau pulled up a straight-backed chair and sat down. "Actually, I've never met the woman. But I know plenty about her from Mary and Bob. Her family is rich, and she helps run the family corporation."

Waylon grinned. "Like I asked, what's so bad about her? Sounds like the kind of woman I would have loved to marry. She could keep me in the manner in which I'd love to become accustomed."

Beau laughed and shook his head. "No way, at least not with this woman. According to Mary, Carolyn Baker doesn't date, and she doesn't have fun. All she does is head up board meetings and make more money. The woman has no heart. Instead she has a gold bar in her chest. If and when I choose to marry, it will be to a woman who has the same values, somebody who comes from the same working-class background as me." Beau leaned back in his chair and frowned. "I don't want her to raise those kids. I know her kind. Her idea of a good upbringing is to send them off to a private boarding school and spend time with them once a year at Christmas.''

"That's not what Bob would have wanted for them boys," Waylon observed.

"Exactly, and that's why I intend to fight to keep them with me." He smiled. "And now that I've got my new help, there's no way the dragon lady is going to take those kids from me. So, what have I missed around here since I've been gone?" he asked, reassured by the thought that the twins were in Carol Cook's capable hands.

"Just a minute!" Carolyn screamed at whoever banged on the front door. God, what now? She grabbed both of the babies from their high chairs, each one clinging to her sides like baby chimpanzees. She hurried to the door and opened it to an older woman who smiled sweetly.

"Good morning, dearie. I've come from the Harrison Agency... about the job?"

For one brief moment, as Trent grabbed a handful of her hair and Brent yanked at her earring, Carolyn wanted to sob in relief and usher the woman inside. Instead, she fought against the urge and drew in a deep breath. "I'm sorry, the position has already been filled."

"Oh, dear, that is a shame. I do so love little boys." The old woman smiled at the kids. "And they look like such sweethearts."

"They are," Carolyn said, certain that Trent was in the process of pulling out enough of her hair to stuff a sofa. Fortunately, Brent had released her earring, sparing her ear. "Now...if you'll excuse me." She didn't wait for a reply. She closed the door, placed Brent on the floor, then tried to salvage what was left of her hair. "Let go, honey," she begged, her eyes tearing as she tried to untangle Trent's iron clasp. She jumped as Brent screamed, an ear-piercing noise that was immediately echoed by Trent. Carolyn gulped gratefully as he released her hair.

She placed both boys in the playpen, picked up half-a-dozen toys that were scattered throughout the room and tossed them into the pen, as well. She threw up a prayer of thanks as they stopped crying and became absorbed with the toys.

Great, now she would have until lunchtime to whip the house into shape. And after lunch there would surely be a nap for the boys. She grinned in self-satisfaction. A piece of cake.

The first thing she had to do was change clothes. A silk suit was not the proper attire for baby watching—although she had a feeling nothing in her suitcase would be appropriate. What she needed was a pair of battle fatigues for spending time in the trenches.

A war. That was exactly what she was involved in, and the enemy was Beau Randolf. His laid-back smile and down-home charm hadn't fooled her a bit. The man was ruthless. He hadn't even given her notice that there was a question of custody for the twins. When she'd learned of Bob and Mary's deaths, Carolyn had reluctantly agreed that the babies were best off with Bob's mother. At least they were with family.

Beau's petition for custody would be decided in court in a few weeks, but he should be receiving word within the week that Carolyn had filed a claim for the twins, as well. Her heartbeat accelerated with the anticipation of the challenge. She would win this battle and take the twins back to New York with her. Beau Randolf wouldn't know what hit him.

She quickly changed into a pair of slacks and a casual blouse, remaining in the living room as she was afraid to leave the babies unsupervised for even a moment.

Terrific, she thought, as she rolled up her sleeves. While they played in the playpen she could make a dent in the mess in both the living room and the kitchen.

She thought of her sisters. Wouldn't they hoot if they could see her now, playing nanny and housekeeper? For the past month, since her brother's disappearance, Carolyn had been acting director for Baker Enterprises, the family corporation. She'd become quite proficient in a boardroom; however, her adeptness in a playroom was yet to be tested.

Carolyn would make whatever sacrifices, rise to any challenge necessary to raise Mary's babies. Mary had been like an additional sister to Carolyn, and Carolyn knew what her friend would want for her children . . . and it wasn't for them to be raised by a man like Beau Randolf.

The morning passed far too quickly. She picked up toys and changed diapers. She folded clothes and changed diapers. She washed dishes and changed diapers. She finally started to worry because there seemed to be more coming out of the boys than there was going in.

By four o'clock she was frazzled. The twins were finally down for a nap and the house echoed with a blessed silence. She'd never imagined that two little creatures could make so much noise. She sank down at the kitchen table with a cup of tea, able to catch her breath for the first time since arriving.

She suddenly realized she needed to call her sisters and let them know about the unexpected turn her trip had taken. Picking up the receiver, she started to call Bonnie, then remembered that Bonnie was in Europe, vacationing while she checked out some leads on Sam's disappearance.

Instead Carolyn quickly placed a collect call to Colleen. Colleen answered, and Carolyn quickly filled her in. "Colleen, stop laughing," she demanded when she was finished the story and her sister's giggles filled the line.

"I can't help it," Colleen sputtered. "You, a nanny and housekeeper... The mind boggles at the very thought."

"Anything would be better for the boys than Beau Randolf," Carolyn retorted. "You should have seen this place when I arrived. Total bedlam."

"And you're going to whip everything into shape?" Colleen laughed again incredulously. Carolyn sputtered an ineffectual protest, falling silent as Colleen continued. "Honey, you're about as maternal as mud. I'm sorry, I just can't believe you think you can pull this off. How are you going to convince Beau that you're a professional domestic? What are you going to do when it comes time to cook?''

"Cook!" Carolyn stared at the clock in panic. "I've gotta go, Colleen. Beau will be home in an hour and a half, and he's expecting a hot home-cooked meal."

They said their goodbyes, and Carolyn looked around the kitchen in consternation. What was she going to do about dinner? She hadn't thought about taking anything out of the freezer to thaw, and the sparse contents of the refrigerator certainly didn't spark any ideas.

She pinched the bridge of her nose, aware of a headache pounding intently right in the center of her forehead. Dinner. *Come on, Carolyn. You're smart.* "You'll think of something," she mumbled as she paced the length of the kitchen. She smiled suddenly, an idea blossoming where her headache had been.

Beau walked into a clean living room and the smell of roast beef lingering in the air. He looked around the room. The toys were all in the playpen, the stacks of clothes had disappeared. He grinned. He'd hired a miracle worker. "Hello?" he called out.

"In the kitchen," Carol answered.

He hesitated in the doorway, taking in the scene before him. The twins were in their high chairs, and they broke into toothy grins as he walked in. At the sight of their smiling faces a warmth of pleasure swept through him. God, how he loved these kids. It almost frightened him, how easily, how quickly they had crawled into his heart.

The table was set with steaming bowls and platters. Carol stood at the stove, her face flushed with the heat. She'd changed out of the suit she'd had on earlier and now wore a pale pink blouse and burgundy slacks. He couldn't help but notice the colors looked nice on her.

"Hi, rug rats," he greeted the kids, touching Brent's nose and ruffling the fine hair on Trent's head. "Anything I can do to help?" he asked.

"No, it's all ready." She poured the gravy she'd been stirring into a bowl, then set it on the table. "Well, let's eat," she said.

Beau nodded and slid into his chair as she sat down across from him. "Wow, I feel like I've died and gone to heaven," he observed as he eyed the meal. "I have to confess, I figured it would take you a couple of days to get things under control, but it looks like you've worked miracles already."

She smiled and handed him the platter of roast beef. "Never underestimate the power of a woman," she said lightly, then frowned as he filled the twins' plates with mashed potatoes and green beans. "I have their food in the microwave."

"I always feed them table scraps for dinner. They're growing boys and need more than that pureed, strained stuff." He grinned as they squashed the potatoes between their fingers. "Although they do need a little work on their table manners." He laughed as a clump of green beans hit the floor, then sobered slightly as he realized she wasn't laughing. "Uh...I'll help clean up the mess after we eat," he offered.

She shook her head. "That's what I'm here for."

"Yeah, but I realized over the last week that having twins is too much work for any one person. I have a feeling it's going to take some real teamwork to keep on top of things."

"Have you considered that perhaps raising the boys is too big a task for a single man?" she asked.

"I've considered little else," he admitted slowly. He frowned thoughtfully, remembering all the nights he'd spent soul-searching on what was the best course of action for Bob and Mary's kids. "Right after their parents' accident, it wasn't an issue because the boys were at Iris's. She's a wonderful woman, lives just a couple of blocks from here. I thought that settled it, but here they are and here they'll stay."

"Yes, but are you sure you can give the boys all they need?"

Beau sighed, wanting nothing more than a change in the topic of conversation. In truth, he wasn't sure of anything. "All I really know is that out of all the options, I'm the best bet for seeing that these boys are raised healthy and happy."

"And what about this dragon lady you mentioned earlier?"

"Ah, the dreaded New York dragon." Beau laughed. "She's the godmother of the twins. I'm positive she'd make a horrible mother."

"Why?"

"She's quite wealthy. According to Bob and Mary, she was raised by governesses and nannies. What could a woman like that possibly know about raising babies?" He shook his head, his jawline tense with determination. "I'm sure she's spoiled and selfish and completely shallow. She couldn't even take the time to come out here for the baptism. I'll die before I'll see those boys with her.''

Carolyn bit down hard on her tongue to keep from asking him if he felt mysteriously ill. "Perhaps she won't seek custody of them.''

"Oh, she'll seek custody,'' he said with an assurance that grated on her nerves. "She's stubborn as a mule and perverse beyond belief. I'm sure she's spoiled as hell and is accustomed to getting her own way. Besides, if nothing else she'll want custody just to see that I don't get what I want.''

Unsure how to answer him, she focused on the twins, who had managed to smear mashed potatoes and green beans in their hair, across their faces and down the front of their clothes. Their food was not confined to themselves, but was also scattered on the floor around their high chairs.

She sighed inwardly. The floor needed to be mopped after every meal. She didn't have to worry about waxy buildup; the linoleum would be covered with food long before it showed signs of stress from too much wax. I only have to deal with all this for a couple of weeks, she thought to herself. Surely in that time she could gain all the ammunition she needed to use against Beau Randolf in a custody battle.

She certainly didn't want a long, drawn-out custody suit, knowing that it would only hurt the boys. And she didn't want the kids just to best him. Her desire for custody went deeper than that and was much simpler. She wanted what was best for them . . . and it wasn't best for them to be here with him. He acted like it was a sin to be wealthy, like she was less of a person because she had money. As far as she was concerned, it was a simple fact. She was in a better position to give the boys the best of everything. Besides, they needed her.

Casting a covetous look at Beau, she wondered why he hadn't been snagged into marriage by some woman. He was physically attractive enough to garner interest from any unattached females in town. Of course, he wasn't her type at all. He was too bold, too handsome...too male. Actually, she knew why he didn't have a wife. Mary had told her Beau was a man who liked playing the field. Love 'em and leave 'em. Just what the world needed, a Casanova raising two boys.

He grinned at her—a lazy, sexy smile that caused heat to rise to her cheeks as she realized he'd caught her studying him.

"Good dinner," he observed, helping himself to more of the roast.

"Thank you," she answered. She fought against a wave of guilt and wondered if he recognized the roast beef as the same they served at the diner on Main Street. The guilt battled with pride. Actually, she considered it a stroke of genius that she'd even thought about the local diner solving her dinner dilemma. She'd called them, arranged for delivery of a complete meal and placed it on her charge card.

Never underestimate the power of a woman. She smiled, eminently pleased with herself.

Beau finished eating and scooted his plate aside with a satisfied groan. "I'm going to have to get back into my jogging regime so I don't gain a hundred pounds if you keep cooking like this."

"Oh, you jog?" For some reason she'd expected him to get his exercise from lifting beer bottles to his mouth. She should have guessed he did something a little more effective. There didn't seem to be an ounce of fat on his body.

"Before the twins came, I jogged two miles every morning. I have to admit, I sort of miss it."

"Now that I'm here, there's no reason why you can't take it up again." Carolyn stood and began to clear the table. "Please, you don't have to help," she protested as Beau grabbed several of the platters. "This is my job."

"We need to get one thing straight," he explained as he continued to clear the table. "In this household, there is no 'my job' and 'your job,' there's just a sharing of the chores that need to be done. The twins create too much work for any one person." He grinned—the devastating smile that immediately caused an uncomfortable flutter in the pit of her stomach. "I think we're going to make a great team."

Carolyn smiled thinly. She would only be on his team as long as it served her purpose. No matter what happened, she had to remember that he was her enemy.

Within minutes they had the table cleared and Carolyn knew she couldn't put it off any longer. The twins needed a bath, now more than ever, with green beans and mashed potatoes decorating their faces and hair. "Could you take Trent into the living room and put him in the playpen?" she asked. "I'm going to give Brent a bath."

"It works better if you just go ahead and put them both in the tub together. They cry when separated and that way you only have to go through the bath experience once instead of twice."

"Bath 'experience'?" She looked at him curiously.

He smiled. "You've got to see it to believe it. You go run the water in the tub and I'll get them ready."

What could two babies possibly do in a bath? Carolyn wondered as she went into the bathroom and turned on the water. Reluctantly she admitted he was probably right about bathing them together. She'd noticed throughout the day that the moment they were separated from each other they wailed in angry protest. Did all twins have that kind of connection to each other, or had the death of their parents bonded them abnormally close?

As she waited for the water in the tub to fill, she turned and found herself staring at her own reflection in the mirror above the sink. For a moment she didn't recognize herself. The makeup she had meticulously applied that morning was long gone. Her hair hung to her shoulders in complete disarray. She'd always heard women with children glowed. But she looked exhausted. Nothing glowed about her except the end of her shiny nose.

She whirled around as Beau came through the door. He'd removed his shirt, baring his broad, bronzed chest, and he carried a naked little boy in each arm. She eyed him resentfully. He had more glow than she did. And why had he taken off his shirt?

Bending down, she turned off the water and tested it to make sure the temperature was all right. She got on her knees next to the tub as Beau placed the two boys in the water, facing each other. "You might want to scoot back a little," he suggested.

"I prefer being this close in case one of them falls," she returned, wishing he would either leave or put his shirt back on. The bathroom seemed to have grown smaller since he'd come in. He nodded and leaned against the sink, a lazy smile lifting the corners of his mouth.

She directed her attention back to the two in the tub. They babbled to each other and then, as if on cue, their arms and legs began to flail. Water flew everywhere and their delighted giggles filled the room.

Water sluiced over Carolyn's face and splashed the front of her, soaking her from the top of her head to her knees.

As she swiped her sodden hair out of her eyes, she heard Beau's chuckle. "I warned you," he said.

She scooted back from the tub, where the twins still splashed with glee. "Do they always do this?"

"Always. They love the water. I think they're destined to become Olympic swimmers." His gaze flickered down the front of her and his smile faded. "Uh, I'll just go grab a couple of towels."

Carolyn frowned, wondering what had caused his hasty exit. She looked down and found the answer. Her pale pink blouse was plastered against her. The water had turned it nearly transparent and not only were the lacy details of her bra evident, so were her nipples. A blush crept its warm fingers up her neck and across her face. She plucked at the wet material, pulling it away from her, mortified by the intimacy she'd inadvertently shared with him. She focused her attention back on the boys, who had exhausted themselves and finally quit splashing.

When Beau returned to the bathroom he was relieved to see her bent over the side of the tub, washing Trent's hair. Good. He didn't need to get another glimpse of her sexy breasts thrust impudently against the wetness of her blouse. That one look he'd gotten had been enough to whet his appetite—an appetite he couldn't indulge without enormous consequences. He couldn't jeopardize things by developing a healthy case of lust for his housekeeper.

"Call me when you're ready to pull them out," he said, realizing that while thinking of how he mustn't allow himself to lust after her, he'd been focused on the inviting jiggle of her rear end.

He left the bathroom and walked into the living room, where he drew in a deep breath. He smelled the scent of lemon furniture polish. That's what she was here for: to clean his house and care for the twins.

He had to make sure his household was in order should a custody battle ensue. He would keep his lust under control. He couldn't afford to screw this up. He would do whatever it took to keep the wicked witch from back East from getting those two little boys.

Chapter Three

Finally, the boys were in bed. Their room was softly illuminated by a night-light as Carolyn tucked them in. She covered up Trent, then laughed when he kicked his legs to displace the blanket. He grinned up at her and kicked his legs again, as if he enjoyed making her laugh. "You little scamp," she said, then leaned down and kissed him softly on the cheek. His sweet baby scent wrapped around her, evoking a warmth in her heart.

Oh, how easy it would be to lose her heart to these little guys. She hardened her resolve to make sure she was the one who raised them. She *owed* it to Mary, but she *wanted* it for herself. They needed a mother, not somebody who would parade a succession of women through their lives.

Beau was right about one thing. She had been raised by nannies and governesses. She'd had everything money could buy, except the feeling of being loved. She hadn't even gotten close to her siblings until the past couple of years. She'd never felt as though she belonged anywhere, with anyone.

Now she had the chance to have the family she'd always dreamed of, and she wasn't about to let it slide through her fingers. She intended to give these boys everything she'd had—and the intangible things she hadn't possessed. Beau could never give these kids the things she could. Not only could she give them their hearts' desires, but she intended to give them all the love that was trapped deep within her heart. Beau could never love them as much as she would.

She left Trent's crib and moved to Brent's. He sat up in the center of the bed, looking at her expectantly. "What's the matter, baby?" She gently laid him down, but he immediately sat up again.

"He's probably just waiting for his bedtime story."

She turned to see Beau silhouetted in the doorway. She noted with irritation that he was still bare-chested. Did the man not own enough shirts? She would like to think that the only way he achieved the flat, defined condition of his stomach was by holding his breath until his face turned blue. Unfortunately, that didn't seem to be the case. "Bedtime story?" She looked at him curiously.

"I tell them one every night." He walked into the room and eased himself into the rocking chair between the two cribs. Carolyn moved over to the door, wondering what sort of bedtime stories this man would tell.

"Once upon a time there was a little girl named Red Riding Hood," he began, the chair squeaking in rhythm as he rocked back and forth. "One day her mother asked her to take some things to her grandmother's house. As she walked through the woods, she stumbled across a house that belonged to the three pigs."

Carolyn frowned. "That was Goldilocks...and the house belonged to the three bears," she corrected. Honestly, the man was simply unfit to be a parent.

The creak of the rocking chair stopped momentarily. "Are you sure?"

"Positive."

He resumed rocking. "Okay, there was Goldilocks, and she stumbled on these houses owned by the three bears. There was a house of straw, one of sticks and another made of bricks."

"Uh, that was the three little pigs," Carolyn interrupted again.

"I thought you said it was the three bears."

Carolyn sighed. The man was hopeless. Utterly hopeless. "It doesn't matter," she said, suddenly exhausted. It had been the longest day of her life. "I'll just go clean up the mess in the bathroom." She had a feeling that before the story was over he would work in a beanstalk and a boy named Jack.

She did a cursory cleanup in the bathroom, wiping down the errant water, then throwing the towels into the hamper. She consciously refused to meet her reflection in the mirror, knowing she probably looked as frazzled and exhausted as she felt. By the time she was finished, she met him in the hallway.

"All's quiet on the western front," he said softly.

"They're already asleep?" she asked in surprise.

He nodded. "My stories seem to have a soothing effect on them. How about a cup of coffee?"

She hesitated. What she really wanted was sleep. It seemed like months ago that she'd left New York, although it had only been that morning. The most grueling meeting with stockholders had never worn her out like she was at this moment.

"Come on," Beau urged. "I'll not only make the coffee, I'll even wash the cups when we're finished."

She nodded, deciding that perhaps over coffee she might gain more information that she could use against him. After all, that's what she was here for — ammunition. And the sooner she got that ammunition, the quicker she could be out of here and back to her civilized life in her Manhattan apartment.

"Besides," he continued as they walked toward the kitchen, "we really didn't get much of a chance to talk about the details of the job this morning." He directed her to a chair at the table, then started making the coffee. "I suppose you expect a day off each week. Will Sunday be okay?"

She bit back the impulse to protest that she didn't really need a day off. She didn't want to do anything that might make him suspicious. "Sundays will be fine."

The coffeepot gurgled and the kitchen filled with the aroma of the fresh brew. Carolyn rubbed her forehead tiredly. A slight headache nagged just above her eyes, reminding her that she'd spent most of the day without her glasses on.

"You aren't from Casey's Corners." It was a statement rather than a question. He poured two cups of coffee, then joined her at the table.

"No, I'm from a little town in Iowa." It wasn't exactly a lie. She had been born in Iowa, but her family had moved to New York when she was a year old.

"Do you have family?"

"No, just a few distant cousins." Carolyn sipped her coffee. Oh, what a tangled web we weave, she thought, uncomfortable with the lies that were necessary to keep him from identifying her as the "dragon lady." What if the agency called him to find out why he hadn't hired the woman they'd sent? Guilt battled with worry and she quickly pushed it all out of her head. She was already committed to what she had done. She couldn't back out now. If the agency called, she would handle it—one way or another. "What about you? Are you from Casey's Corners?" If they talked about him, she wouldn't have to lie.

He leaned back in the chair, balancing on the rear two legs. "Born and raised here. Never wanted to be anywhere else."

She looked at him in surprise. She didn't think she'd ever known anyone who'd never dreamed of life in another place. As much as she loved New York, there were times she wondered if she wasn't missing something. "Casey's Corners seems like a nice little town."

"It's a wonderful place to raise two boys." He reared back a little farther in the chair and Carolyn averted her gaze, once again overly conscious of the expanse of his bare chest, of the springy dark hair that decorated the center, then crept down his flat abdomen to disappear into the top of his slacks. Didn't somebody's etiquette book say it was offensive to sit at a table without a shirt? She added abhorrent table manners to her mental list of his deficiencies.

"What about you? Any family?" she asked.

He shook his head and returned his chair to its upright position, his eyes dark and somber. "No. I was an only child and my parents passed away a couple of years ago. I always considered Bob, the twins' father, as the brother I never had. We grew up together and were really close until he got a wild hair and moved to New York. He met Mary there and got married, then I convinced them to move back here." He gazed off in the distance for a long moment. "Thank God I got those last two years with them."

Two years that Carolyn hadn't had with her best friend. Two years of life and laughter that had been stolen from her. A stab of resentment coursed through her as she thought of the time she'd lost with Mary — time stolen from her by Beau's manipulation of Bob in offering him a job here. Her own grief rose up in her throat, tasting bitter.

"Anyway," Beau continued, "I have my family now . . . those two little boys in there."

Carolyn finished her coffee, suddenly needing to be away from this man and his attractive chest. "I assume since the boys are in bed, I'm off duty?"

He nodded.

"Then if you don't mind I think I'll go to my room. I didn't get a chance to unpack yet." She rose from the table, exhaustion tugging at her once again. "I guess I'll see you in the morning." As he murmured good-night, she left the kitchen.

She walked into the bedroom that would be her home for the duration of her stay and stifled a groan. Everything from the living room that she hadn't known what to do with, she'd thrown in here.

Her bed was buried beneath a pile of clothes she hadn't had time to fold, the foam containers that din-ner had arrived in sat accusingly on the top of the small dresser. All she wanted was to fall into bed and dream peaceful dreams where no children cried, no food was thrown and all men wore shirts—a safe, comfortable dreamworld where she was in control. She'd felt horribly out of control all day.

Bending down, she opened her suitcase and pulled out her nightgown. She would deal with the mess to-morrow. All she wanted at the moment was sleep. Undressing and pulling her nightgown over her head, she shoved everything off the bed, turned out the light and crawled beneath the sheets.

Her body instantly conformed to the unfamiliar contours of the mattress, too tired to fight the un-comfortable lumps. Caring for the two boys had been more work than she'd anticipated. It was just that she wasn't accustomed to this particular kind of work, she assured herself with a yawn. She'd walked into a sit-uation and coped the best she could in the hours she had, but tomorrow would be different. Tomorrow she would be in complete control.

She rose back up, spying a clock radio on the night table next to the bed. Moving the alarm hand, she set

it to go off at five. That should give her a comfortable jump on the day. She would be able to get some
of the housework done before the twins woke up.

Lying back down, she released a deep sigh. Despite
her tiredness, her thoughts turned to Beau Randolf.
He didn't fit the image she'd had in her mind of him
before arriving here. For one thing, he was much more
attractive than she'd anticipated. She'd expected a
beer-bellied, swaggering Neanderthal who lived in a
shanty with disabled cars in the front yard. She hadn't
expected a man with dark, tumbled hair that beckoned her fingers to dance through it. She hadn't expected a man with a drop-dead gorgeous smile and
eyes that sparkled with sinful thoughts.

There had been a softness in those eyes when he'd
spoken of the twins as his family; a softness that had
touched her deep inside.

She punched the pillow, irritated by the direction of
her thoughts. It didn't matter that he was attractive.
It didn't matter that he'd looked all soft and appealing when he'd talked about family.

He was wrong for the boys. This town was wrong
for the boys. Mary's boys deserved the very best, and
the best certainly couldn't be found in a place called
Casey's Corners and with a man like Beau Randolf. In
New York they would have the kind of opportunities
that couldn't be found here. They would be exposed
to so much more. A single woman could raise children far better than a single man.

As always, in the last moments before sleep claimed
her, Carolyn thought of her father's murder and her
brother's resulting disappearance. Her father, Jo-

seph, had been shot and killed in his office at Baker Enterprises. The police suspected Sam of the crime. Carolyn knew better. Although Sam and her father had often argued vehemently about business, Sam wasn't capable of such a heinous crime. So, where was he? Why hadn't he faced the accusations, defended himself? What, other than death, could possibly keep him away from his wife and little girl?

Although Carolyn kept in close contact with her sister-in-law and niece, she missed her brother, needed to find out what had happened to him. What could he possibly have been doing here in Casey's Corners? And if he had been in town, where had he gone from here? Punching her pillow a final time, Carolyn drifted off to sleep.

Brent's and Trent's familiar cries pierced Beau's sleep. In the past week, he'd grown accustomed to being awakened in the middle of the night. Since their arrival at his home, the twins had yet to sleep through an entire night.

He started to get up, then remembered that Carol Cook was now in the house. It was her job to care for the boys. That's what he'd hired her for. He relaxed once again and waited for sounds that would indicate Carol was up and taking care of the boys. Moments passed and he tensed as the cries continued, growing louder.

When there was still no noise from Carol's room and the cries were loud enough to raise the entire neighborhood, Beau got out of bed and yanked on a pair of jeans. He passed Carol's closed bedroom door and went into the next room, where both Trent and Brent stood in their cribs, hanging on to the rails and crying lustily. He turned on the overhead light, unsurprised when their tears magically stopped and they each gave him a toothy grin.

"You're both a couple of little fakes," he said, laughing as he picked up one and anchored him on one hip, then did the same with the other.

He wasn't sure why they awoke each night. Sometimes their diapers were wet, sometimes dry. Sometimes they wanted a bottle, sometimes they didn't. It was as if what they really needed most was a little middle-of-the-night reassurance and love.

After checking their diapers, he carried them into the kitchen and situated them in their high chairs, then gave them each a vanilla wafer to gnaw on. In his week of experience, he'd found that after a cookie and a little conversation the boys usually went back to bed without a fight, for the rest of the night.

"So what's happening, fellows?" he asked, slumping into the chair nearest their high chairs. They both grinned, drooling over the cookies in their mouths. He remembered the night they had been born. He'd been in the waiting room with Bob. He'd paced the floor next to him, jumping each time the waiting-room door opened, wondering if this time it would be the doctor. Finally, when the labor was over, Beau had passed out as many cigars as Bob.

He smiled as he recalled Bob's relief when Mary had announced she didn't want him in the delivery room. Bob had confessed to Beau that he didn't want to be there. He'd been afraid he would disgrace himself by passing out. Beau had thought his friend was crazy. He remembered thinking at the time that when his wife had their children, he wanted to be there at her side, reminding her to breathe, sharing every moment of the miracle of birth.

His smile wavered. A lot of good it did him to think about the birth of his children. He wasn't anywhere near getting married, hadn't even dated anyone special in over a year. The little town of Casey's Corners had everything he wanted, except an abundance of eligible single women.

He stifled a yawn with the back of his hand, wondering what in the hell he was doing sitting in the kitchen in the middle of the night when he had a woman he'd hired sleeping in the spare bedroom.

Unable to believe that Carol had slept through the noise, he stood. "I'll be right back," he said to the two cookie monsters. At Carol's bedroom door, he knocked softly, wondering for the first time if everything was all right. She should have gotten up with the kids.

He knocked again, louder. When there was still no answer, he frowned worriedly. He suddenly realized he didn't know anything about her. What if she was a secret drinker? Or hooked on sleeping pills? What if she was an escapee from a mental institute? Sure, the agency he'd used was supposed to have an intensive screening process, but he knew there were people who slipped through the bureaucratic cracks all the time.

He knocked once more, and when there was still no answer, he twisted the knob and opened the door. Moonlight spilled through the window and onto the bed, painting Carol in shimmering silvery illumination. She was on her back, tiny ladylike snores escaping her parted lips.

Her dark hair was splayed across the white of the pillowcase and her features were soft with dreams. The sheets were tangled around her middle, exposing not only the thrust of her breasts beneath the filmy midnight-blue nightgown, but also the shapely length of her bared legs. As Beau stared at her, he felt his stomach muscles tighten and clench in response.

He could tell by her breathing that she was deeply asleep, and for a moment he entertained the thought of playing Prince Charming to her Cinderella. He wanted to lean over and kiss her softly parted lips and see if that would awaken her from her hundred-year sleep. He frowned. Or was it Snow White who had slept for a hundred years?

It didn't matter. He wasn't about to kiss her and wake her up. She'd performed miracles today in completely cleaning up the living room, taking care of the boys and providing a delicious dinner. She was obviously exhausted, and she'd earned the right not to be disturbed.

He turned away, pausing as the light from the hallway spilled onto the dresser. Then he spotted several containers from the diner. He recognized them because he'd often had Wanda, the owner of the diner, send something home for him to warm up in the microwave.

He grinned. So, his miracle worker hadn't worked such a miracle, after all. No wonder the evening meal had tasted like Wanda's advertised "home cooking." It *had* been her cooking.

His grin widened as he spied the gold glint of a credit card lying next to the empty cartons. So, she'd charged dinner and had it delivered. She'd probably wanted to make a good impression on him. He found this oddly endearing.

He reached out and picked up the credit card, his fingers moving over the raised letters of her name. Carolyn Baker.

His heart stopped for a moment. Leaning back so the light of the hall shone fully on the card, he read her name again. Carolyn Baker. "What the he—"

He glared at the woman lying there asleep, fighting the impulse to grab her by the hair and drag her out of bed. What the hell kind of game was she playing?

He thought over the morning, for the first time vaguely remembering the confusion on her features when he'd greeted her and thrust a kid in her arms. He'd just assumed she was the woman from the agency, and he'd made it incredibly easy for her to seize that role. Grudging admiration for her flared up inside him. She'd seen an opportunity and grabbed it. He couldn't fault her for that.

He carefully placed the credit card back exactly where he'd found it, then gazed once again at the sleeping woman. So, this was the wealthy dragon lady from New York. Trent and Brent's godmother.

What was she doing here? Why on earth had she spent the day pretending to be Carol Cook? Hell, he could arrest her for impersonating a housekeeper.

He grinned again, knowing he was going to do no such thing. He didn't know what she was up to, but he liked the idea of her being right here under his nose where he could keep an eye on her. Quietly, he left her room, closing the door once again.

Going back out into the kitchen, he sank down in one of the chairs and raked a hand through his hair thoughtfully.

"Ga-ga-ga." Trent banged on the high-chair table and absently Beau handed him another cookie.

He'd expected her to turn up sooner or later, although in his wildest dreams he hadn't anticipated she would be sleeping in his spare bedroom.

There was only one reason why she would have come. She wanted the kids. Well, tough. He smiled again, his blood surging with the anticipation of battle.

"This could get real interesting, boys." With a wide smile still lingering on his lips, he handed the boys another cookie and told them the story of the three billy goats gruff and the big bad wolf who wanted to blow their houses down.

Chapter Four

Carolyn flung a hand out to shut off the alarm. Without opening her eyes, she rolled over onto her back. It had to be a mistake. It couldn't be time to get up already. It felt as though she'd just gone to sleep minutes ago. She couldn't remember the last time she'd been so tired.

She didn't want to get up. Snuggling back under the covers she closed her eyes once again. She just wanted to remain here in bed and fall back into her dreams of a tanned, broad chest, a chest she'd been kissing, the springy dark hair pleasantly tickling her lips. A chest that had been warm and inviting, a chest that— She sat up, appalled as she remembered the dream she'd been having before the alarm had interrupted.

She'd been touching, caressing, kissing a masculine chest—not just any chest, but Beau's. She'd obviously been exhausted into insanity. She swung her legs over the side of the bed and glared at the alarm clock, as if the instrument were personally responsible for the early hour and her crazy dreams.

Fortunately her room had a connecting bathroom and after springing out of bed and standing beneath the hot spray of the shower, she emerged feeling almost human. She dressed quickly, then went into the kitchen, turning on the light against the predawn darkness. She groaned as her shoe slid over a green bean from the night before. She had to do something about the floor. But first, coffee.

She set about making the coffee, then leaned against the counter as it dripped through the brewer and into the glass carafe. She hoped Beau didn't expect her to cook him breakfast. Back home in the luxury apartment where she lived, she had both a cook and a housekeeper to take care of the daily chores. The closest Carolyn got to cooking was zapping a frozen dinner in the microwave on the weekends when her cook was off duty.

She poured herself a cup of the fresh brew and sank down at the table, savoring the quiet surrounding her. She wondered how long the quiet would last. Were the twins early risers?

After spending yesterday tending to the children, she had come to the conclusion that once she got them back to New York, she would probably have to find another place to live. A penthouse apartment just wasn't right for raising a couple of boys. Perhaps she could buy a house near her sister-in-law, one with a large backyard and a swing set. Eventually the children would need a place to run and jump and grow.

She would probably have to hire a nanny for those days when she had to be at a meeting. She'd always poured her energies and talents into the family business and since Sam's disappearance, the demands on her time had increased.

Certainly she would check nanny references more closely than Beau had. It was appalling how easily he'd allowed her into his home without knowing a thing about her. What if she'd been an ax murderer? A child abuser? Surely the judge would agree that Beau Randolf was lax in his duties and totally unacceptable as a guardian.

Finishing her coffee, she stood and eyed the floor with disgust. Time to get to work. Who knew how long she had before everyone woke up?

She found a bucket and a bottle of ammonia under the sink and got to work on the gritty floor. She couldn't help but think about what she would be doing if she was back home. She certainly wouldn't be scrubbing a floor.

After a few minutes of work, Carolyn sat back on her haunches and eyed the portion of the floor she'd just scrubbed. It was unbelievable what a little soap and water could accomplish. A warmth of pride flooded through her. Odd, how such a mundane act could produce such a positive feeling.

"Good morning."

She jumped and spun around at the sound of Beau's voice. He stood, clad in a pair of jogging shorts, his bare chest a reminder of the crazy dreams she'd had the night before. "Morning," she murmured, leaning over again and continuing her work.

"You're very industrious this morning," he observed.

"I thought it might be a wise idea to get a jump on the day," she said, continuing to scrub an additional area of the floor. She didn't want to look at him—not with her dream still so fresh in her mind, not with his chest still so bare to her gaze. "What time do the kids usually get up?"

"It depends on how long they're up in the middle of the night. If they aren't awake for long in the night, then they usually are up between six and six-thirty. If they're awake for a long period of time in the night, then they sometimes sleep until seven-thirty or eight. It should be a later morning today."

She stopped and turned back around to look at him. "They were up in the middle of the night?"

He grinned. "Apparently you're a very sound sleeper."

"I'm sorry, I should have heard them." Reluctantly she stood. "I didn't know what time you got up so I haven't done anything about breakfast—"

"Don't worry about it. I'm not a breakfast eater. I usually just grab a cup of coffee before work." He looked at his wristwatch. "If I'm going to get in a morning jog before I go to the station, I'd better head out." He walked to the back door. "I'll be back in about a half an hour." He paused a moment, his grin wide. "Although I must admit your rear end has the cutest wiggle when you work, I think it only fair that I tell you there's a mop inside the pantry closet."

He disappeared out the door before Carolyn could vent a growl of frustration. She'd cleaned half the floor on her hands and knees with a mop resting snugly in the closet. And what right did he have to check her out while she worked? Oh, he was proving to be exactly what she'd thought he was—a male chauvinist who would raise her godsons to be little miniatures of himself. God forbid.

She finished the floor with the mop, her irritation driving her to scrub long and hard. When she was finished, she looked over the results with a sense of pride. "So there, Colleen," she said aloud, thinking of her sister's laughter the day before. "I told you I could handle all this."

After washing her hands and cleaning out the bucket, she poured herself another cup of coffee and sat down at the table. Outside the window she could see the first stirring of dawn as it stretched gold and pink hues across the horizon. Summer was just around the corner. She smiled, thinking of the boys out on the beach, playing in the sand as the ocean lapped the shore. Casey's Corners and Beau Randolf certainly couldn't give the boys an ocean. She could.

She looked up as the object of her ire returned, out of breath and perspiring. "Whew, not even fully daylight yet and it's already getting hot. I think it's going to be a long, hot summer." He walked over to the sink and filled a glass with water.

Carolyn noticed that the sight of his bare back was equally as attractive as his chest. Wide and tanned, with sinewy muscles, she wondered what it would feel like to splay her hands across its width, feel those muscles moving against her fingertips. She watched in fascination as a trickle of sweat trailed languidly down the center of his back and was finally absorbed by the material of his waistband. His skin looked so sleek, so shiny...so touchable.

She tore her gaze from him, wondering if she was suffering some sort of ammonia-fume poisoning. Why else would she be thinking about caressing Beau's back?

He finished drinking his water and looked around. "Wow, the floor looks terrific. I'd forgotten that it had blue flecks in it. Like your eyes." With another of his enigmatic, irritating grins, he left the kitchen.

A moment later Carolyn heard the water running in the bathroom, indicating that he was taking a shower. She hoped he drowned. Before she could fully enjoy her vision of Beau going under for the third time, she heard a cry from the boys' bedroom. A new day had officially begun.

Beau stood beneath the stream of hot water from the shower, unsure which he found more pleasurable—the tingling spray on tight muscles, or the mental vision of Carolyn Baker scrubbing the floor, her rounded derriere wiggling provocatively.

He knew it was bad, knew it was absolutely rotten of him to get such pleasure out of the fact that the wealthy, pampered, haughty socialite had cleaned his kitchen floor.

How long would she continue the charade? How far could he push before she cried uncle and confessed her real identity?

Although he found her shenanigans amusing, what he didn't find humorous were the stakes in this game they played. He had to admit he admired the lengths she was willing to go to for the children, but he wasn't about to allow her to win.

He and Bob had spent long hours talking about Trent and Brent. Beau had heard all of Bob's dreams for his boys. Beau knew the most important ingredient in their upbringing was love, and he loved them completely, unconditionally, without complication.

Even Mary had admitted that she didn't want the boys raised the way she had been raised. Mary had come from a privileged background and for a while she and her blue-collar husband had tried to live that life-style. Bob was appointed head of security in Mary's father's firm at a yearly salary that was as much as Beau expected to make in his entire lifetime. But it wasn't long before Bob and Mary decided they wanted something different and had come back to Casey's Corners for a simpler, less stressful life. Bob and Mary had agreed with something that Beau had known all his life: that money couldn't buy happiness.

He wondered if Carolyn Baker had any concept of that notion, wondered if she had any values except material ones. He didn't want the boys raised by strangers, sent away to schools, raised with everything money could buy but without the values, happiness and love money couldn't acquire.

There was no doubt in his mind that he would be a wonderful father for Trent and Brent, that he could teach them morals and values far more important than fancy clothes and cars. Besides, he could give them love, and he wasn't sure Carolyn knew the real meaning of that word.

He shut off the water and stepped out of the shower. One thing was certain. He hadn't expected to be attracted to the dragon lady. Carolyn Baker might be the wrong woman to raise Trent and Brent, but she definitely sparked a physical response in him.

Yes, indeed. It would be interesting to see how this played out. There was definitely a perverse part of him that enjoyed shaking her up. He'd enjoyed the way her eyes had widened when he'd mentioned her rear end, the way her lips had compressed tightly when he'd commented on the blue of her eyes.

Carolyn Baker appeared to him to be a woman who needed to be shaken up. There was a shell of cool reserve surrounding her that taunted him, enticing him to break through and discover what sort of woman was beneath. She seemed surprisingly unaware of her own sex appeal, as if she'd spent plenty of time being the head of a corporation, but very little time just being a woman.

Minutes later, dressed in his deputy uniform, he went back into the kitchen, surprised to see the twins dressed and seated in their high chairs. His heart warmed as they kicked their legs and wiggled their bottoms in excitement at the sight of him. He kissed them each on the forehead, aware of Carolyn's narrowed gaze on him as she stirred two bowls of instant oatmeal. He also noted that a bedsheet was now spread beneath the high chairs. "Pretty ingenious," he observed.

She shrugged. "It's easier to wash a sheet than it is to scrub the floor."

He nodded his agreement and poured himself a cup of coffee. He leaned against the counter and watched as she positioned a chair between the two boys.

As she alternated spoonfuls of oatmeal to each of them, a ray of sunshine streaked in through the window and painted the three of them in a warm, golden glow. Trent reached out a chubby hand and grabbed a strand of her sun-kissed hair. Trent laughed, Carolyn laughed, and the sight of her smile-softened features, the sound of her husky laughter caused Beau's stomach to clench in pleasure. He realized it was the first time he'd seen her smile, the first time he'd heard her provocative laughter; and the fact that he found both so enjoyable suddenly irritated him.

He finished his coffee and grabbed his car keys from the counter. "I'll see you tonight," he said, then left the house and headed for work.

As he drove to the police station, he thought again of how she and the boys had looked in that golden light spilling in the window. It had been like something out of a Norman Rockwell painting, a scene depicting life and love. Mother feeding the children while father looked on with pride. Anyone peeking in the kitchen window at that moment would have guessed they were a family. But it was a fraudulent image.

Carolyn Baker—Carol Cook—was in his home under false pretenses. She didn't want to be a part of his life. Instead, she wanted to take part of his life away with her. He couldn't forget that, even for a moment. Despite the fact that her smile had shot rivulets of warmth through him, despite the fact that her laughter had pulled a resulting smile from him, he had to remember she was his enemy.

He pulled into his reserved parking space in front of the station and shoved all thoughts of Carolyn Baker out of his mind.

The day passed in a flurry of paperwork. Beau had two deputies who worked for him and he knew the time was fast approaching when he would have to hire a new man. Casey's Corners was growing instead of fading into the dust like so many of the small towns in Kansas. Unfortunately, along with the new people who joined the community came additional crime.

It was almost time for him to head home when Waylon entered. He hitched his pants up, then sank down into the chair across from Beau's desk. "Gave out two speeding tickets this morning."

"Ah, a day in the life of a crime fighter."

Waylon grinned. "Thought I was going to have to arrest old Mrs. Baskins. When I gave her the ticket she hit me with her purse. Said she was going to tell my mama that I had no respect for my elders."

Beau grinned. "What did you do?"

"I told her at least my mama respected the speed limit. Mrs. Baskins hit me with her purse once more, then drove off." Waylon grinned and shook his head. "Somebody needs to take her license away. An eighty-seven-year-old speed demon is a menace to society."

"I'll try to get out and talk to her son," Beau said, making himself a note to that effect. "Maybe he can talk her into relinquishing her driver's license, or at least get her to slow down."

Waylon reared back and the chair groaned ominously beneath his weight. "So, how's it going with the new housekeeper?"

Beau smiled reflectively, thinking of the dinner from the diner, the mess he'd spied in her bedroom when he'd gone in to wake her up. He shrugged. "It's too soon to tell if she's going to work out." In fact he knew she wouldn't work out. It was just a matter of time before she called a halt to whatever game she was playing and went back to her own frivolous, indulgent life.

"There's a dinner and dance at the community center this Saturday night. Regina made me promise I'd invite you and the boys and your new housekeeper. Everyone is supposed to bring a covered dish."

Beau grinned at this thought. It might be worth taking her just to see what kind of "covered dish" she would bring. Perhaps he would take her, at that. Beau had always been proud of the fact that Casey's Corners was filled with people who had heart, and no place was that heart more visible than at the occasional Saturday-night gatherings.

"You tell Regina we'll be there," Beau said, making up his mind. Besides, it would be a nice outing for the twins. Immediately following the tragic car accident that had claimed their parents' lives, the townspeople had rallied around the two little boys. People had generously showered Bob's mother with food, sympathy and offers to baby-sit the children at any time.

Beau wanted to show Carolyn exactly what kind of community love and support she was trying to take the boys away from.

He stood, suddenly eager to be home and see how Carolyn's day had gone. He knew as well as anyone how demanding, how exhausting a full day with the boys could be. After giving Waylon parting instructions, he left.

It bothered him, envisioning the life the kids would have if Carolyn somehow managed to gain custody. He couldn't imagine that she would give up her jet-set life-style to be a full-time mother. Of course, the same thing could be said for him. He had his work, which meant the boys would be raised by a housekeeper. On that particular score they were even.

In the best of worlds, he would marry and the boys would be raised in the warmth of a family. Unfortunately, the most serious relationship he'd had was with a woman who had, since they'd broken up, married and had a child of her own. He couldn't even remember now why they had broken up. More, he couldn't remember what had attracted him to her in the first place. There had been a lot of women, a lot of water under the bridge. It had been a long time since he'd been intensely attracted to anyone... until Carolyn Baker.

Beau tightened his grip on the steering wheel, aware that his mind was carrying him into dangerous territory. It did him no good to think of how Carolyn had looked sleeping in that sexy midnight blue nightgown. It did him no good to remember the warmth of her smile as she'd laughed with Trent that morning.

She was his enemy, attempting to wrestle from him the most precious gifts fate had ever given to him. No matter how physically attractive he found her, he had to remember that she was the dragon lady who was interested only in gaining custody of the boys he loved.

He pulled into his driveway, noting that the lawn needed tending. Perhaps he would get a chance to mow this weekend. He didn't know how long Carolyn would keep up her subterfuge, but he intended to take advantage of it. While she was taking care of the kids he could get some work done that he hadn't been able to do before.

As he walked into the house, he was greeted by the scent of meat loaf. It didn't surprise him. It was Thursday, and Thursdays were "meat-loaf special" days at the diner.

He could hear the boys in the kitchen, their fussy cries filling the house. When he entered it only took one look at Carolyn to assess that she'd had a tough day. Her hair was tousled and a vertical frown line etched the center of her forehead. A variety of stains and spills decorated her pastel floral blouse.

Trent and Brent greeted him with squeals that were somewhere between joy and crankiness. "Hi, boys," he said, touching each of them lightly on the top of the head before sitting down in a chair at the table. "Rough day?" he asked Carolyn, who stood at the sink drying dishes.

She hesitated a moment, then nodded. "A little. They didn't take naps today. All they did was drool and cry." She set the dish towel on the counter and rubbed her forehead.

"Headache?"

She nodded again, as if reluctant to admit any weakness. "I should be wearing my glasses more often."

"So why aren't you?"

She looked at Trent and Brent. "They won't let me."

He stared at her blankly. "Pardon me?"

Carolyn walked over to the countertop by the phone and picked up a pair of blue-framed glasses. She slipped them on and looked at the twins. The result was astonishing. Both boys stared at her for a moment, then burst into loud, screeching cries. Beau laughed.

"It's not funny," she protested as she yanked the glasses off. The twins immediately stopped crying. For a moment Carolyn's eyes looked suspiciously damp. Beau was shocked. Dragons didn't cry.

"I think the glasses scare them," Beau explained as she put the glasses back on the counter. "Tomorrow I'll pick up a couple pairs of little plastic sunglasses. Maybe if they play with those, they won't be frightened of yours."

"That sounds like a good idea." She smiled and again Beau noticed how her features softened appealingly. He wondered how many negotiations she had clinched on the basis of that smile. "Thanks," she continued. "I was afraid I had two choices. I could be blind and have a headache or I could wear the glasses and actually see how much I scare them." Her smile lingered for another moment, then she cleared her throat and turned toward the stove. "Supper is ready."

Just as Beau suspected, supper consisted of meat loaf, green beans and mashed potatoes and gravy. Wanda's meat-loaf special. The kids were fussier than usual. They chewed on their fists, rubbed their eyes, drooled and eyed their supper with disinterest.

"I'm worried about the kids," Carolyn said when they were almost finished eating. "I think they're both running a little fever, and they've been really fussy all day."

"I imagine it's nothing more serious than teething," Beau said as he finished the last bite on his plate. "I'll pick up a couple of teething rings tomorrow. In the meantime, we'll put a couple of washcloths in the freezer and they can chew on those. The cold will soothe the irritation of their gums." He smiled at her innocently. "That meat loaf was great. Is there more?"

"More?" She looked at him blankly. A faint pink crept up her neck. "Sorry, I don't have any more. It was a very small loaf."

You are a wicked man, Beau thought, as he watched the blush completely sweep over her features.

Carolyn got up from the table and began clearing the dishes from the table, her face still a soft, distinct pink. "Next time I'll make sure it's a bigger loaf," she said.

He looked back at the boys, whose fussing had risen in volume. "I'll make you a deal," he said as he stood. "If you'll take care of the kitchen, I'll get these guys ready for bed. You said they didn't have a nap, and they act like they're tired."

"It's a deal," she replied. She watched as Beau swung each child up into his arms, then disappeared down the hallway. She breathed an instant sigh of relief. What a day. She didn't understand it. She'd been caring for the twins for two days, and she was still waiting for the glow.

It was all so much more complicated than she'd originally thought it would be. There was so much more work, and the children demanded so much time and attention. How did mothers do it? How did they keep a spotless house and still give what was needed to the children?

She'd managed to keep the living room and the kitchen relatively clean, but her bedroom had been unofficially designated as the catchall room, and things were really piling up in there.

Teething rings, frozen washcloths... How did Beau know so much about children? Why did it all seem to be so easy for him? The twins positively squealed with delight each time he walked into the room.

She finished clearing the table and put all the dishes in the dishwasher. Pulling the sheet up off the floor, she took it to the back door and shook it, then placed it beneath the high chairs again.

Of course, things would be different when she got the boys back to New York. She could hire a proper, well-trained nanny to care for them during the day and she would devote her evenings to them. They would have two aunts who would love them to death and all the advantages the big city and her money could offer. Surely she would glow when she finally had them in her own home, accustomed to her routine.

Kitchen cleaned, she went out in the hallway and stood just outside the boys' bedroom doorway. She could hear the low rhythmic squeak of the rocking chair and Beau's deep voice as he told them their bedtime story.

She smiled, unsurprised to hear about Rapunzel sweeping the ashes in a fireplace and caring for her three hateful stepsisters. Again she was struck by how easily he wore the mantle of fatherhood. Most men she knew would balk at the thought of wasting time telling bedtime stories to ten-month-old boys. Of course, most of the men she knew weren't eager to have children at all.

Assuming the story was drawing to an end when she heard him telling them that Rapunzel had pushed the mean old witch into the oven, Carolyn walked back to the kitchen and put on a pot of coffee.

"There's nothing better than the smell of fresh-brewed coffee," Beau said as he returned to the kitchen.

"Unless it's drinking a cup of it," Carolyn added, motioning him into a chair. "They asleep?"

He nodded. "We'll see how long they stay that way. I'm sure it's their teeth that's giving them fits." He thanked her as she poured him a cup of coffee, then joined him at the table.

"How do you know so much about kids?" she asked.

"When I was ten, my mother started baby-sitting in our home. There was always at least one baby either colicky, teething or at some other stage of development." He shrugged and grinned. "Besides, I guess for some of us parenthood just sort of comes naturally.''

Carolyn sipped her coffee, then looked at him with studied nonchalance. "So, how do you know that the dragon lady wouldn't be a wonderful, loving mother to the twins?"

Beau barked a laugh that instantly rankled her. "A barracuda probably has more maternal instinct than that woman," he answered, a grin lingering on his lips.

"How can you know that? Didn't you tell me you've never met her before?" Carolyn was pleased to hear the cool mild interest in her voice.

"I gained a pretty good picture of her from the things Mary told me about her."

"And what kind of things did Mary say?" she asked, fighting to keep her indignation from her tone.

Beau shrugged. "Apparently Mary and the dragon lady had been friends for years. They went to the same fancy private girls' school." He raked a hand through his hair, then paused to take a sip of his coffee. "Mary said she was ambitious, ruled by her need to succeed rather than her heart." He put his cup back down. "I just got a pretty good picture of the dragon lady from the little things Mary said."

"And what kind of picture do you have?"

"Mental or physical?" he asked.

"Both."

He leaned back and tipped the chair on its hind legs, his dark eyes gleaming as if he was enjoying the effects of a private joke whispered in his ear. "Mentally, I think the lady is rigid, so structured that there's no place for spontaneity in her life. She's given all to the family business, running a corporation and immersing herself in her work to make up for the fact that she has no personal life. Away from her family wealth and position, she probably has no self-identity. She's not a woman, she's a corporation. And where her heart should be, there's nothing but a balance sheet.''

Carolyn shifted uneasily on her chair, fighting the urge to kick the back legs of his chair out from beneath him and tumble him to the floor. "And what about her physical appearance?"

His grin was lazy and amused as he gazed at her. "I envision the dragon lady with hair about like yours, although she would never allow it to get so untidy." His grin widened as her hand reached up self-consciously to smooth order to the mussed locks.

"Go on," she said, clenching her hands together in her lap.

He allowed his chair to fall back forward and leaned across the table. Carolyn could smell him, a masculine scent that was instantly appealing. The smell of warm sunshine, fresh air and masculinity. His jaw was dark with the trace of a five o'clock shadow and she wondered if it would be soft, or abrasive against her skin. She leaned back in her chair, needing more distance between them.

"Her eyes are blue," he continued, "Not the warm blue of a summer day, but the frigid blue of icy waters. And her lips are skinny, like wrinkled prunes."

"Prunes?" Carolyn squeaked.

He nodded with an assurance that made her want to smack him upside the head. "Anyone as repressed and bound by duty as Carolyn Baker has to have thin, wrinkled lips from keeping them pursed in haughty distaste all the time."

Carolyn scooted back from the table, unable to rein in her vast irritation with the man, his smug smile and unattractive assessments of her. "She may be structured and rigid and have prune lips, but she probably knows her fairy tales better than you."

Without waiting for his reply, she stomped out of the kitchen and into her bedroom. The mess that greeted her there only made her more angry. Beau Randolf was an opinionated, small-minded, dolt.

She shoved a pile of clothes off the bed and sank down on the edge of the mattress. What was wrong with being structured? She had to be in order to keep her schedule. She'd grown up knowing that her place was working in the family corporation, following in her father's and Sam's footsteps.

She'd worked hard to get where she was, to gain the respect of the men who worked for her. What was wrong with being strong, independent, yet understanding her duty to the family business? All the qualities he'd listed about her were qualities she'd always liked about herself. But, falling from his lips, they had sounded like character flaws.

She undressed, her movements jerky with irritation. Beau was probably the type of man who believed that every woman needed a good old-fashioned roll in the hay. Repressed, indeed. She wasn't repressed. She frowned, realizing her lips were pressed tightly together.

Pulling her nightgown on, she turned out the light and got into bed. Prunes indeed. She punched the pillow, then turned over on her side. Drawing in a couple of deep breaths, she allowed the darkness and the silence to soothe her.

Chapter Five

A covered dish. Carolyn stood in front of the refrigerator and stared blankly at the contents. They were going to a community supper and dance this evening, and Beau had told her she didn't have to cook dinner, but she did need to fix a covered dish to take with them. A covered dish of what?

She sank down at the kitchen table and shoved her glasses up on top of her head. From the kitchen window came the whir of the lawn mower and the pleasant scent of freshly mowed grass. She hoped the noise from the mower didn't disturb the twins' nap. They'd been so fussy the last two days.

Actually she was grateful for the dinner this evening. Since Beau had the day off, she'd worried how she was going to manage the diner delivery of their supper without Beau knowing about it. Now all she had to figure out was what she was going to prepare to take with them this evening.

On impulse she got up and went to the phone. Using her calling card, she punched in her sister's number.

Colleen answered on the second ring. "Carolyn! I've been wondering what's going on out there. Is everything okay with the twins? Have you found out anything about Sam? When are you coming home?"

"As far as the twins are concerned everything is under control. I really haven't had an opportunity to find out anything about Sam." Carolyn rubbed her forehead thoughtfully. "Any news about him there?"

"None."

Carolyn heard the quiet despair in her sister's voice. Colleen and Sam had always been so close. The disappearance had been difficult for all of them, but more so for the youngest member of the Baker family who had idolized her big brother. "Colleen, what I really need from you is a recipe." Stunned silence met her words. "Colleen, don't ask why and don't make jokes. I need a recipe for a covered dish."

"A covered dish of what?"

Carolyn sighed. She should have known better than to ask either of her sisters. Bonnie ate nearly every meal in a restaurant and Colleen was as helpless in the kitchen as Carolyn. "Never mind. It was silly of me to call and ask you."

"Carolyn, why are you trying to fight this battle on unfamiliar grounds? Get away from the housework and cooking before your brain turns to mush. Wait until it gets to court where you can hire a shark and can go for his throat."

For some reason, Colleen's words unsettled Carolyn. She didn't necessarily want to go for Beau's throat. She just wanted custody of the twins. They needed her. "Colleen, I have to do this my way. I don't want to tie this up in court, and I don't want to bankrupt him. The easiest, kindest way to do this is to catalog all the reasons why he shouldn't have custody so the judge will make the proper decision." She closed her eyes and pinched the bridge of her nose. "I'd better let you go. I've still got to figure out something to fix for a dinner we're going to tonight."

"Call a caterer. Surely you can find a place who specializes in hors d'oeuvres of some kind?"

After hanging up with her sister, Carolyn once again stood in front of the refrigerator door. She could just imagine the faces if she took a plate of fancy hors d'oeuvres to serve to a bunch of Kansas farmers. Besides, she had a feeling pâté and caviar would be in short supply in Casey's Corners.

Closing the refrigerator door, she looked at the canned goods, finally deciding that she could bake several cans of beans and throw in some sliced hot dogs. It wasn't creative, it wasn't exotic, but it would be hot and hearty.

With this problem out of the way, she walked over to the window and gazed outside, where Beau pushed the lawn mower across the expanse of the lush backyard.

She'd apologized to him yesterday morning for storming out of the kitchen when he'd been talking about Carolyn Baker. She'd told him she'd been playing the devil's advocate for the absent woman. He'd merely smiled enigmatically.

As she watched, Beau paused with the mower idling. He swiped an arm across his brow, then walked over to where a wooden trellis had fallen on its side. As he picked it up and worked the bottom stakes back into the earth, the tanned muscles of his arms and back glistened and danced with the exertion. She pulled her glasses off the top of her head and perched them on the bridge of her nose where they belonged, instantly bringing him into sharper focus.

She'd never been so physically aware of a man as she was of Beau. She didn't understand it. It wasn't like her world wasn't filled with a lot of attractive men. She worked with nice, confident handsome men in power suits and ties. But none of them radiated the kind of raw masculinity that Beau emitted so effortlessly. None of them made a coil of heat unfurl in the pit of her stomach.

Uttering a sigh of disgust, she turned away from the window. The very last thing she needed was to develop a case of the "hots" for Beau Randolf. She wanted nothing to complicate her ultimate goal. Besides, once Beau discovered who she really was, the playful, warm light in his eyes would darken to anger and enmity.

She jumped as the back door opened and he walked in. She realized the noise of the lawn mower had stopped.

"Boys still asleep?" he asked as he opened the refrigerator and grabbed a bottle of orange juice.

She nodded and watched as he flipped the plastic lid off the juice and tipped the bottle to his lips.

He drank deeply, his Adam's apple moving as he swallowed. Carolyn had a sudden desire to press her lips against the dark hollow of his neck, taste the salt of his skin, feel the pulse point throbbing against her cheek. Her own mouth was suddenly cotton dry.

He finished drinking and held the bottle out toward her. "Want some?"

She flushed, irritated with herself and her errant thoughts, even more irritated with him. "That's disgusting." She grabbed the bottle from him and placed the lid back on the top. "You shouldn't drink out of the bottle like that."

"That's what my mother always told me."

"And have you always done the opposite of what your mother told you was right and proper?" She put the juice back into the refrigerator.

"Only when I thought it might be more pleasurable than not." He stepped closer to her. "I listened to her for the important things. For instance, I never run with scissors in my hands, and I don't put anything smaller than my elbow in my ears."

Again he stepped closer to her and the cool surface of the refrigerator pressed against her back as the heat that emanated from him warmed the front of her. "But there are some things mothers tell you not to do that you just have to try—like eating raw cookie dough, drinking out of the milk jug and skinny-dipping when it's far too early in the year and the lake is cold."

He stood so close to her now, she could feel the warmth of his breath on her face, see the tiny silver flecks that softened the dark gray of his irises. His voice was unusually deep and affected her like a caress. Her breath caught in her chest as he leaned toward her and braced his hands against the refrigerator on either side of her, effectively capturing her in an almost embrace. "Tell me, Ms. Carol Cook, didn't you ever do anything your mother told you not to do?" His mouth was so close to hers. "Haven't you ever done anything that you know isn't quite proper, but instead is delightfully wicked?"

She suddenly felt disoriented as a flame of anticipation burned deep down in the pit of her stomach. He had a beautiful mouth with full, sensual lips that looked velvety soft. She wanted to taste them, feel them dancing across the line of her jaw, down the length of her throat. She closed her eyes to steady herself against the sudden rocket of desire that shot through her.

"Aren't you going to go get them?"

She opened her eyes and blinked, fighting against the fog of longing that surrounded her. "Wha-what?"

"The boys... Remember them? Trent and Brent?"

She realized he'd dropped one of his arms and had stepped back from her. She also saw that the playful smile that had curved his lips and sparkled in his eyes only a moment before, was gone.

Squeals of impatience came from the twins' room and she spiraled back to reality with a small gasp. "Yes... I'll just go get them," she muttered, scooting out of the kitchen as her cheeks burned hotly.

As she changed Trent's diaper, she berated herself, wondering how on earth a simple discussion of manners had turned into such intense yearning for his kiss. As she changed Brent's diaper, she mentally berated Beau for being so damned sexy.

"Another day or two... that's it," she said, propping one child on one hip and one on the other. Within another day or two she should have more than enough ammunition to fight Beau in a custody suit. In the meantime, she would just have to make sure she didn't put herself in a position where she wondered about Beau's kisses again.

"Hey, buddy, that's a no-no." Beau grabbed the decorative vase before Trent's inquisitive hands could reach it. He diverted the little boy's attention with a handful of blocks, then looked at his watch, wondering how much longer Carolyn would be.

She had bathed and dressed the children, then Beau had offered to sit with them while she got ready. He eased back down in his chair. As he watched the kids playing in the middle of the floor, his thoughts drifted to that moment in the kitchen when he'd almost thrown caution and good sense to the wind and kissed her.

It had been a close call. Had the boys not awakened and yelled, who knew what might have happened? His mind suddenly filled with a vision of him making love to Carolyn on the kitchen floor, her long sexy legs wrapped tightly around his hips. He smiled, remembering the way her eyes had flared, their blue darkening as her lips had parted to invite his kiss.

He leaned back in the chair and rubbed a hand thoughtfully across his lower jaw. He was going to have to call an end to this game soon. Contrary to everything he had ever thought possible, Carolyn Baker was definitely getting under his skin.

An affair with her, no matter how fleeting, would only complicate what already promised to be a complicated matter. With or without the twins, eventually she would go back to her life in New York and he would remain here.

Still, when he'd leaned into her against the refrigerator, her scent had whirled in his head, removing all reason. Her soft, moist lips had beckoned him to taste, to plunder their sweetness. She'd even closed her eyes, as if anticipating his kiss.

With a low growl, he stood and restlessly paced the room, needing the physical activity to cool his blood. Maybe it was time he looked more closely at the single women in Casey's Corners. He'd dated hot and heavy during the years before Bob and Mary had moved back to Casey's Corners, but he'd never found anyone who made him think in terms of "forever."

Perhaps his physical reaction to Carolyn was only a reflection of a natural biological clock of sorts telling him it was time to seriously seek a wife. Before Bob's and Mary's deaths, Beau had sated his hunger for family by being a part of theirs. Mary had constantly nagged him to find a nice woman and settle down. "Bimbos, that's all you date," she'd accused.

Since the boys had entered his life, he hadn't even considered seeing any of the women he had dated in the past. They had been terrific for a few dates, but they weren't mother material.

A marriage would probably tip the scales of justice in his favor when it came to the custody of the boys. Unfortunately, it would be impossible for him to get married before the judge made his decision.

As Trent grabbed his lower leg, Beau grinned and bent down to pick the boy up in his arms. "My mama always said I was a perverse cuss," he said to the child, who smiled and reached to grab his nose. Most men got a wife before they had the children, but not Beau. He'd always done things the hard way.

He smelled Carolyn before she actually walked into the living room. The scent of her soft, utterly feminine perfume preceded her and caused the flame in his groin to renew its burn.

He turned toward the hallway in expectation, at the same time trying to break Trent's death grip on his nose. "Let go, kid," he muttered.

As she entered the room, he forgot all about his nose being wrenched. Gone was the frazzled caretaker of twin boys, and in her place was a lovely woman in a pale blue dress. The dress molded to the thrust of her breasts, hugged tightly to her slender waist, and danced in flirtatious folds around her hips. It was long enough to be decent, but short enough to display what seemed to him an indecent length of slender, sexy legs.

"Is this all right?" She stood hesitantly, her hands nervously working down the sides of her skirt.

He set Trent on the floor and straightened, trying to keep his gaze off those legs. "I must say, you clean up right nice."

Her hair was pulled back and caught at the nape of her neck with a gold barrette, and small hoop earrings winked on the lobe of each ear. Her makeup was subtle, enhancing the peach of her cheeks, the lush color of her lips and the dark length of her lashes. She looked cool, elegant—every inch the wealthy lady he knew her to be. This thought irritated him.

"Come on, we'd better get going or we're going to be late," he said gruffly. He pulled a double stroller out of the hall closet and unfolded it, wrestling for a moment with the cumbersome contraption. "I thought we'd walk to the community center. It's only a couple of blocks and it's a pretty evening."

"Sounds like fun," she agreed. She picked up Trent and put him in the stroller while Beau grabbed Brent and did the same. "They look so cute in those matching outfits."

Beau nodded, looking at the two in their identical baseball shirts and pants, their only difference the color of their socks. A river of grief welled up in his throat and he swallowed hard against it. "Bob bought those for them the day they were born. He said before he and Mary were through, he hoped they had enough kids for an entire ball team."

She touched his arm and as he gazed at her, he saw his pain, his grief reflected in her eyes. He realized the loss was not his alone; that she grieved for the couple, too. Surprisingly, it helped. He cleared his throat and she dropped her hand from his arm. "So, let's hit the road."

"Wait! My beans." She hurried into the kitchen with Beau following closely behind.

As she pulled the casserole dish out of the oven, he looked at the contents, then grinned at her wryly. "Old family recipe?"

She returned his smile. "Not my family."

Within minutes they were on their way, the casserole dish resting well beneath the twins' feet, along with two diaper bags and an assortment of toys.

As Beau had indicated, it was a pleasant evening. A mild breeze, fragrant with sweet spring scents, stirred the trees that lined the sidewalk. The boys had awakened from their naps in good moods and they cooed and jabbered in the secret language of babies.

Carolyn looked forward to the evening out. After spending the last three days with nobody to talk to except the twins, she was hungry for adult interaction—although not quite as adult as what had almost happened between her and Beau before the twins had interrupted them.

She cast a furtive glance at him as they walked leisurely down the cracked sidewalk. His jeans hugged his long legs with easy familiarity and the short-sleeved T-shirt displayed tanned forearms and bulging biceps as he pushed the stroller. How was it possible for a man to look so damned sexy when doing nothing more than pushing a couple of drooling, babbling kids?

Instead of looking at him, she focused her attention on their surroundings, noting the neat, attractive houses they passed along the way. Had Sam walked these same streets? Had Mary been mistaken in thinking she saw him? What could have brought him to the small Kansas town?

She shoved these thoughts away, knowing she couldn't ask questions as long as Beau thought she was Carol Cook. Carol Cook wouldn't know or care what had happened to Sam Baker. Just a day or two longer, she promised herself, then her charade would be over and she could delve fully into the mystery of Sam.

Insects buzzed and clicked, as if celebrating the deepening shadows of twilight. "It's nice that there are still some places left where people can walk the streets and not worry about their safety," she observed.

He nodded and smiled. "Casey's Corners is a place where kids still play outside, where the teenagers do drive-by mooning instead of drive-by shootings."

Carolyn laughed. "As deputy sheriff, you must take a lot of pride."

"I do. This town has a lot of heart, and I like to think I have something to do with that." A frown usurped his pleasant smile. "Casey's Corners is growing by leaps and bounds and that worries me a little. I'd hate for it to grow so big the heart could no longer be found."

Carolyn thought about Manhattan. It had lost its heart long ago. Too many people, prevalent crime and too much fear dictated that people kept to themselves, went about their business without connecting with others. Carolyn had lived in her apartment building for two years, but she didn't know any of the people who shared the building with her.

She frowned, realizing she favored Casey's Corners as the town where she would prefer the boys to be raised. Okay, so Casey's Corners won in this respect, but there were many, many more things to consider.

"There isn't much in the way of cultural activity here, is there?"

He looked at her in surprise. "I guess it depends on what you consider cultural."

"Museums, the opera, theatrical productions— things like that."

"Once a year the high school puts on a dynamite theatrical production, and Ralph Watson, our resident barber, sings a mean aria when he's had one too many beers. As far as museums go, Ben Walker charges a dollar a head for a tour of his barn where there are more relics from the past than you've ever seen in one place."

Carolyn frowned. A high-school play, a drunken barber and an old barn weren't exactly what she'd had in mind as cultural enlightment. "Besides driving around and mooning people, what on earth do the teenagers do with their time on weekends?"

Beau stopped to pick up a rattle Trent had dropped. He rubbed it on his jeans, then gave it back to the little boy. "We've got a movie theater and a bowling alley, and lots of times they have parties in the cemetery." He laughed at Carolyn's shocked expression. "There's no better way to get a girl to cuddle with you than by frightening her in the darkness of a cemetery." His laugh faded and he looked at her soberly. "Actually, we've got a good bunch of kids here, raised with strong parental support and values and plenty of love. Besides, there's no place in this town that kids can go and misbehave without somebody seeing them and threatening to tell their parents."

As they rounded a corner the community building came into view. More than a dozen cars and trucks were parked out front, and the sounds of talking and laughter drifted out the open door. Carolyn's nerves unexpectedly tingled with anxiety. It was one thing to misguide Beau as to who she really was, quite another to mislead an entire town. In for a penny, in for a pound, she thought. The welfare of Trent and Brent was worth any subterfuge necessary.

When they entered the building, greetings immediately overwhelmed them. Beau introduced Carolyn to the many people who came to coo at the boys, and her head spun with new names and faces.

It wasn't until the supper officially began that she finally had time to assimilate and put names to faces. She and Beau sat at the end of a long picnic table, the boys happily playing in and eating a conglomeration of food on their stroller trays. The cacophonous din in the room made it difficult for her to hear Beau as he tried to tell her a little something about each of the people in the room.

She leaned closer to him as he pointed out Ralph Watson, the baritone barber. Beau put his arm around her shoulders, drawing her nearer as he told her that not only did Ralph sing in the shower, but he also was sleeping with Margaret Benton, the lady who owned the local floral shop. "Even though Ralph and Margaret pretend there is nothing going on between them, people have been making bets at the post office as to when he'll be singing his arias in Margaret's shower."

"How can you know all these people's secrets?" she asked incredulously. In the last few minutes Beau had told her who was sleeping with whom, who was a closet drinker. He seemed privy to all kinds of information.

He smiled, his gaze holding hers for a long moment. "There are very few secrets in Casey's Corners."

For a moment Carolyn's heart jumped and skipped a beat. Did he know? Was he aware of her duplicity? Or was the erratic beat of her heart a reaction to the warmth of his arm around her shoulders, his evocative scent that surrounded her, the closeness of his lips to her as he whispered in her ear?

She leaned away from him, breathing in relief as he dropped his arm from around her. "I am so stuffed," she said, pushing her paper plate away. "I've never seen so much food all in one place."

Beau smiled. "One thing all the folks in Casey's Corners have in common is a love of good food. Your bean casserole was a hit." His smile faded as he looked past her. Carolyn followed his gaze to see an older woman entering the room. "Excuse me." Beau got up and hurried toward the woman.

Beau hugged her, then stepped aside as others came up to greet her. A few minutes later, Beau escorted her toward Carolyn and the twins. As they drew closer, Carolyn noticed that the left side of the woman's face sagged and her gait was slightly uneven. Her left foot dragged as if without energy and her left arm hung limp at her side.

"Carol, I'd like you to meet Iris Johnson, Bob's mother and Trent and Brent's grandmother."

Carolyn stood and her hand was clasped warmly by Iris. "It's so nice to meet you. Beau has told me what a help you've been with the children." Iris's blue eyes teared as she looked past Carolyn to where the twins sat in their stroller. "And there's my babies."

She released Carolyn's hand and bent down to the boys, who broke into toothless, drooling grins as she cooed to them. "Oh, they look wonderful." She struggled back up and smiled at Beau and Carolyn. "I think every day they look a little bit more like Bob. Don't you think so?" she asked Beau. Carolyn heard the grief in Iris's voice, the need for continuity between her beloved son and the two little boys in the stroller.

"Yes, they look a lot like Bob," Beau agreed softly. He placed an arm around Iris's thin shoulders, their mutual fondness evident.

"I'm so grateful the children weren't in the car with Bob and Mary when the accident occurred." She looked back at the twins, her eyes teary. "I don't know what I would do if I'd lost all of them."

Beau gave her shoulder a squeeze. "Trent and Brent are lucky to have a grandma as loving as you."

Iris smiled gratefully at him, then reached a hand out to take Carolyn's. "And between the three of us, we're going to see that those boys grow up right here in Casey's Corners, right?"

"Right," Beau instantly replied.

Both of them looked at Carolyn. She smiled and nodded vaguely, a sick feeling in the pit of her stomach. Taking the boys away from this town, away from Beau and Iris, was definitely going to be more diffi-

cult than she'd initially anticipated. For the first time
since she'd arrived in Casey's Corners, Carolyn wondered if she was doing the right thing.

Chapter Six

"Come and dance with me," Beau said to Carolyn. The supper was officially over and the picnic tables had been pushed toward the sides of the large room to provide a dance floor in the center. A three-piece band had set up and several couples were already dancing to the country tune they played.

She looked at the twins. "Come on, Iris will watch them while we dance," he said, effectively stifling the protest he knew she was about to voice.

"Go on," Iris urged. "I'll be more than happy to sit here with the boys." She shook a rattle and both boys laughed in delight.

Beau reached for Carolyn's hand and pulled her out among the other couples who were dancing to the beat of the music. "I don't know how to dance this way," she protested.

"It's just an easy two-step," he assured her. "All you have to do is follow me." He pulled her into his arms and realized this was what he'd been waiting for all night long, an excuse to hold her close.

Her perfume filled his senses, muddled his thoughts as he allowed himself to fall into the pleasurable sensation of her body close to his. The material of her dress was cool to his touch, but he could feel the heat of her body radiating beneath it. Her hair smelled nice, like springtime flowers on an apple tree.

"You dance very well," she said after a moment.

He smiled down at her. "Don't sound so surprised. Even us country boys know how to cut a rug on the dance floor."

"You're a man of many talents."

"You've only seen a few of them." His smile widened as a soft blush swept over her features and she averted her gaze from his. There was something about her that seemed so untouched, so innocent. "Aren't you interested in some of my other talents?"

"I don't think so." Her voice sounded a little breathless as she kept her head averted.

Beau liked the way she sounded when he managed to shake her up. He wondered if she'd emit breathless sighs when she made love? He wondered if husky moans would escape her lips when she was caressed? He stopped these thoughts, aware that his body was responding in a distinctly physical way to the heat of his erotic visions.

"One of my talents is that I can whistle all of the theme song to 'The Andy Griffith Show.'"

"I told you I wasn't interested in your hidden talents," she replied, but a small smile danced at the corner of her mouth.

God, she was so beautiful. He found himself wanting to watch that smile sweep completely over her features. He wanted to hear the smoky laughter that warmed him from the inside out.

"I can also carve an apple to look like Abraham Lincoln," he continued, wanting desperately to make that tiny smile widen. "And I sing a mean rendition of 'Blue Suede Shoes.'"

She laughed and a thrill coursed through him. "You're crazy," she exclaimed.

He nodded. "I am. Now tell me some of your secret talents."

She shook her head as the song they'd been dancing to came to an end. "Ah, too late. The dance is over."

As the band began a slow ballad, Beau pulled her back into his arms, this time so close he could feel the press of her breasts against his chest. "Not so fast," he protested. "I can't let you go until you confess your secret, hidden talents. After all, it's only fair since I bared mine to you."

She laughed again, but didn't try to leave his embrace. She frowned thoughtfully, causing an endearing wrinkle to furrow her brow. "I can swim the length of a swimming pool underwater without taking a breath."

"No big deal. So can I."

Her frown returned as she gazed at him thoughtfully, then smiled. "I can cross only one eye."

He looked at her skeptically. "Only one?"

She nodded and as he watched, her left eye drifted to the center, then straightened once again. As he laughed, she flushed and shook her head. "I can't believe I'm doing this—standing in the middle of a dance floor crossing one eye." She laughed, a pleasant sound that rolled over Beau like a cool breeze on a hot summer night. "You're a bad influence on me."

Beau smiled and pulled her closer against him. He had a feeling he was a good influence on her. She was far too serious, far too intense too often. A little uninhibitedness was good for the soul. "You know we'll be the talk of the town tomorrow," he murmured softly.

"Just for dancing together?" She looked up at him again, her eyes a wide, brilliant blue.

"It doesn't take much to start talk." He remembered all the gossip that had drifted though town about him when he'd been dating a lot. According to the local talebearers, he'd been having an affair with every woman he took out for a cup of coffee.

All too soon the dance came to an end and Carolyn moved out of his arms. As she walked back over to where Iris sat with the twins, Beau was stopped by Waylon.

"You lucky dog, you," Waylon said, his gaze following Carolyn as she sat down next to Iris. "She's a real looker."

"She is pretty, isn't she?"

"Regina is dying to meet her."

Beau smiled, knowing Waylon's wife was one of the town's most prolific gossips, but a woman with a heart of pure gold. "Bring her over and I'll make the introductions."

Moments later, after Beau had introduced Regina and Carolyn, he leaned against the wall, his gaze scanning the crowded room. He saw Verna Walrick dancing with one of the Bellamy brothers. She smiled and winked at him. He smiled back, one without promise.

He'd been considering asking Verna out before the twins had come to live with him. He watched the buxom blonde twirling on the dance floor and realized he had no desire whatsoever to ask her out. Everyone knew that Verna didn't want to get married. She was having too much fun.

He frowned, thinking back over the women he'd dated. Funny, he'd always gravitated toward the women he knew didn't want a long-term relationship. Mary used to tease that because he was such an important part of their family, he had no need to have a family of his own. But he knew the single thing that had kept him from marrying so far was fear. The fear that his own relationship wouldn't live up to the glowing examples he'd been given in his life—first his parents, then Bob and Mary. He'd seen the best of relationships and would settle for nothing less for himself.

What scared him now was that since Carolyn Baker had moved into his home, there was no other woman in the town of Casey's Corners who sparked even a minute interest. Throughout the evening he had looked at all the single women in the room, and realized that none of them did a thing for him—none of them except Carolyn.

It's nothing more than a bad case of lust, he told himself firmly. He turned his gaze to where Regina and Carolyn were in the middle of an animated conversation. Carolyn used her hands effusively as she talked, and he tried to imagine her in a boardroom making decisions that generated dollars. Unfortunately, all he could see was a mental image of her sleeping in that damned sexy nightgown.

Lust, he thought again. He certainly wasn't a stranger to the cravings of lust. But it had been his experience that the best way to deal with lust was to sate it. And once sated, it quickly disappeared.

He didn't entertain any thoughts of a future with her. With or without the twins, eventually Carolyn would go back to her life in New York. They were from different worlds, lived completely different lifestyles. He was certain their values, their desires, their dreams were completely opposite. The only thing they had in common was the fact that both of them wanted the boys.

It was just after ten o'clock when Beau decided it was time to get the children home. They were fussy, obviously overstimulated and overtired. Carolyn seemed to read his mind. The moment he looked at her, she nodded and began packing up the diaper bags.

"It might take more than a bedtime story to get these guys settled down tonight," he observed moments later, as they started the walk home.

"They both seem overtired," she agreed.

Overhead the stars beamed down brilliant light and a full moon peeked out from behind an errant cloud. Beau breathed deeply of the cool night air. It was spiced with all the scents of small-town living. It was the smell of green pastures, and the lingering odors of home cooking. "Beautiful night," he commented. He watched as she drew in a deep breath, a pleasant smile lingering on her lips.

"Hmm, it smells so clean."

Beau merely nodded. God, she was beautiful with the moonlight stroking her features and making her eyes shine with a luminous light. She was softer, warmer, so much more alive than he'd imagined in all his previous thoughts of the formidable Carolyn Baker.

She's just hiding her prickly side, he told himself. She's playing a role for my benefit. In reality she has no heart, no real soul. Making money, that was what the Bakers did, and there was little time for anything else in their lives.

Still, in the moonlight, with a soft smile on her lips, Carolyn looked like a woman with enormous heart. She looked like a woman he could love.

Inwardly he scoffed at the very absurdity of his thoughts. Apparently the moonlight was addling his brain. Love, indeed. He didn't even know if he liked Carolyn Baker. Hell, he didn't know the real Carolyn Baker. He only knew this facade, the pretend woman named Carol Cook.

He sighed in relief as his house came into view. He needed to get out of the moonlight, before his crazy thoughts went any further.

As soon as they were inside, chaos reigned as Beau and Carolyn worked together to get the boys into their pajamas. The kids fought back, flailing their legs and whining fitfully. "They're definitely overtired," Beau said, finishing with Brent and placing the cranky child in his crib. He moved over to help Carolyn with Trent.

"He's a slippery little worm," she said as Trent tried to crawl away from her, his diaper half on, half off. Beau captured him and placed him where Carolyn could finish dressing him. When she was finished she placed him in his crib, where he pulled himself up to a standing position and stared at Beau and Carolyn with accusing eyes.

"Go to sleep, baby," Carolyn said, trying to lay him down, but he popped back up again like a jack-in-the-box.

"They might need to cry themselves to sleep," Beau said.

Carolyn turned to look at him in shock. "Cry themselves to sleep? We can't let them do that."

"Why not? It doesn't hurt them. In fact, it's good for their lungs."

"I don't care. That's heartless." She leaned back over Trent's crib and stroked his little face softly. Although there were no tears, Trent continued a fitful, fussy crying.

Beau touched Carolyn on the shoulder. Seeing her so maternal did strange things to his heart, and he suddenly wanted her out of the room, away from the kids. "You can go on to bed if you want. I'll tell them a story and sit in here until they fall asleep."

"I don't mind sitting up with them," she protested.

"I realize that, but one of us needs to be rested in case they awaken later in the night. You go on to bed and I'll take care of them now."

She looked at him hesitantly. "You won't just let them cry themselves to sleep?"

"I promise I'll sit in here until they go to sleep." With a final kiss to each of the boys' foreheads, Carolyn left the room. A moment later he heard the soft click of her bedroom door being closed.

He sank down in the rocking chair between the two cribs, his thoughts still on Carolyn. She was probably taking off that pretty dress now, and pulling on the sexy blue nightgown. She'd stand in front of the dresser mirror and unclasp the barrette at the nape of her neck, allowing her hair to fall to her shoulders. He closed his eyes, imagining her brushing her hair, the nightgown slipping to expose a silky shoulder.

A fire ignited inside him, a fire that burned deep in his veins as his imagination tormented him with visions of her.

He could see himself sliding the nightgown from her shoulders as he kissed the smooth, sweet skin of her neck. His palm tingled with the illusion of cupping her breast, tracing down the slender lines of her stomach, seeking the heat of her—

"Ouch!" Beau grabbed his forehead, then looked down at the floor where a plastic rattle now lay at his feet. Trent laughed and bounced up and down.

"Did you throw that?" Beau grinned at the little boy. "I think you have a future as a pitcher." He rubbed his forehead once again, grateful for the interruption of his previous thoughts. He needed a rattle upside the head to keep erotic thoughts of Carolyn at bay.

"How about a story?" Beau rocked in the chair, the familiar low creak filling the room. "Once upon a time..." he began.

Carolyn tossed and turned, unable to drift into sleep despite the fact that she was exhausted. Her mind whirled, refusing to allow her the oblivion of sleep.

For the very first time since receiving the letter telling her that Beau Randolf sought custody of the twins, Carolyn had doubts concerning her own plan to take the boys from here.

Going to the dinner and dance had been a mistake. She hadn't wanted to see Casey's Corners as a loving, giving community, and yet that's exactly what she had seen. She'd felt the warmth of the people—people who had accepted her completely, without reservations. There hadn't been a single person there who hadn't taken at least a moment to bend down and talk to the babies, tickle them under their chins, then place a kiss on their foreheads.

With a sigh of irritation, she plumped her pillow and tried to find a body position that would evoke sleep. But her mind wouldn't shut down.

Her mind filled with a vision of Iris. Bob's mother—the grandmother of the twins. Carolyn's heart ached as she thought of the woman who had lost her son and daughter-in-law; a woman who obviously loved the kids to distraction. It wasn't going to be easy taking the children away from her, whisking them to a city over a thousand miles away.

I can buy her plane tickets, she thought, trying to still the guilty, nagging voice inside her. She can come to New York and visit whenever she wants. I could always pay for Iris to relocate to New York City. I'll make certain she gets to see the children as often as possible, she mentally promised.

No matter how difficult, she had to make her decision based on what was best for Brent and Trent. And damn it, she was best for them. They needed her. She could give them the finest her money could buy.

She sighed, remembering her own childhood. She'd had the finest money could buy. Materially she'd never wanted for anything—except the knowledge that she was loved, the certainty that she was special to her parents.

I won't make the same mistakes with Trent and Brent, she vowed. Shoving any other disturbing thoughts away, she closed her eyes and waited for sleep.

She didn't realize she'd fallen asleep until she woke up and looked at the luminous dial on the clock. Three in the morning. She sat up, wondering what had pulled her from her sleep. Then she heard it, the faint cry of one of the boys.

Immediately she got out of bed and hurried into the boys' room, where Brent stood crying. "What's the matter, honey?" she asked, quickly picking him up and cuddling him close against her. She checked Trent, who still slept peacefully, apparently undisturbed by his twin's cry. She carried Brent into the kitchen.

She turned on the small light above the stove, then grabbed a bottle from the refrigerator and popped it in the microwave. When the bottle was warm, she sat down in a chair at the table, the little boy still cuddled close against her. "Shh," she soothed him, stroking the feather down of his hair, smelling the sweet baby scent that clung to him. He drank from the bottle, making little sounds of contentment as she rocked him back and forth. He held the bottle with one hand and with the other he reached up to touch her face. His touch was whisper soft and she kissed the tiny hand as her heart filled with a love she'd never before experienced.

Such a tiny little person, she thought, marveling at the perfection of the chubby hand. In the best of worlds, it would be nice if the twins could have both a mother and a father, a loving unit to raise them together. Her own parents had always seemed like distant strangers. They'd rarely come into the children's quarters of the house and Carolyn couldn't remember a time her mother had tucked her into bed or told her a story.

She hummed softly, an old lullaby from her own childhood that her favorite nanny had often sung to her. Brent smiled around the nipple of the bottle, milk dribbling down his chin.

"Looks like double duty."

She looked up to see Beau standing in the doorway, a tear-stained Trent in his arms. "I didn't even hear him," she said in surprise.

"Looks like you've got your hands full." He walked over to the refrigerator and took out a bottle. As it warmed in the microwave, Carolyn averted her gaze from him. He was clad only in a pair of red cotton boxers and she was suddenly aware of the brevity of her own attire.

The microwave dinged and he sat down in the chair next to hers, Trent cradled in his arms. "Here you are, tiger," he said, as Trent latched onto the bottle and thrust it in his mouth. Beau smiled at Carolyn—a conspiratorial smile that instantly put her at ease. "I wonder when these two are teenagers if they will still be getting up in the middle of the night for a snack?"

Carolyn smiled and once again rubbed the soft hair on Brent's head. "At least when they're that age we won't have to get up with them."

"Who would have thought that there would be a time when I'd spend my days putting butts in jail, and my nights putting butts in diapers?"

She laughed softly. "Did you always want to be in law enforcement?"

"Always. I don't remember ever wanting to be anything else." He smiled and cuddled Trent closer against his broad chest. "My mother used to say that instead of being born with a silver spoon in my mouth, I was born with a gold badge on my chest."

"You were close to your parents?"

"Yeah." In the faint illumination of the kitchen his eyes glowed with painful memories. "My parents were terrific. I had a wonderful, happy childhood. I was eighteen years old when my father died in a freak tractor accident. My mother seemed to lose the will to live after that. A year later she passed away in her sleep from a massive heart attack. That's when I started spending a lot of time with Bob and Iris. They became my second family.''

"She seems like a wonderful lady," Carolyn said.

"She's the best. She was nearly heartbroken when Bob moved to New York for job training. Then when he married Mary and started working as head of security for a big firm, Iris feared she'd lose touch with him. We were both so pleased when he and Mary moved back here.'' He sighed and leaned down and kissed Trent's forehead. "At least they left a legacy behind.''

Never had Carolyn seen Beau look as appealing as he did at this moment, with a child cuddled against his bare chest and a soft light of love shining from his eyes.

All of this would be so much easier if he'd truly been the Neanderthal she'd expected him to be. If he'd been a beer-guzzling, belly-scratching lowlife, she would have suffered no compunction about using any means necessary to take the boys away from him. But it was going to be difficult to take the boys away from this man.

She hardened her heart against Beau, refusing to allow herself to be swayed from her goal, and her goal was to do what was best for the twins. And they needed her.

For a few minutes the kitchen was silent except for the ticking of the clock on the wall above the stove and the sounds of the bottles whistling as the boys worked at draining them.

She became aware of Beau's gaze on her. Where moments before he had been introspective, thoughtful, his gaze now lingered on her, bringing a flush to her cheeks as she felt the heat contained in his eyes. It wasn't the look of a man for his housekeeper. It was the look of a man for a woman, full of fire and hunger.

She gripped Brent closer against her, as if he could shield her from the flood of warmth that suffused her, the unexpected desire that rose up inside her as if in answer to his. Never had she felt so feminine, so wanted, as when she looked into his eyes.

Bedroom eyes. She was receiving the full force of his bedroom eyes, and it both frightened her and excited her in a decidedly uncomfortable way. She'd never felt these feelings before. She hadn't had much experience in the dating arena. There had never been time.

Looking back down at the baby in her arms, she realized he'd fallen asleep. Take him back to his bed, then escape into your own room, a little voice instructed deep inside her head. Get away from Beau with his hot eyes and sexy smile before you do something stupid.

Drawing in a deep breath, she suddenly recognized what she felt. She glowed. She could feel it on her face, sensed it throughout her being, saw it reflected in Beau's eyes. Sitting here in a semidark kitchen, holding a sleeping baby who held on to one of her thumbs, she shimmered, she shone... she glowed.

She stood, achingly aware of her intimate attire. "I—uh—I'll just put him back in bed." She fled the room as if the hounds of hell were nipping at her heels. However, the hounds of hell wouldn't be capable of making her body tingle as if every nerve ending was exposed.

It wasn't the babies that made a woman glow, it was the desire of her husband that created the ethereal radiance on a woman's face.

As she placed Brent in his bed, alien thoughts jumbled her head. She'd always believed Mary had somehow sacrificed herself, marrying so young instead of forging a place for herself in the business world.

Mary had been intelligent and energetic, and Carolyn hadn't been able to imagine how a man and a family could fulfill her. Now Carolyn found herself wondering if Mary hadn't been smart, after all.

What was so great about Carolyn's life? Sure, she did a fine job as acting director of Baker Enterprises, but other than her two sisters and brother, she had nobody to share the triumphs, nobody to kiss away disappointments, nobody to share her dreams. She was successful and alone. She frowned and turned away from the crib, stifling a cry as she saw Beau standing in the doorway.

"Shh." Beau gestured to the sleeping child in his arms. She watched for a moment while he placed Trent in the crib, then she turned and went out into the hallway. She hadn't quite made it to her bedroom when Beau stopped her, calling her name and standing directly in front of her.

"I forgot to tell you about another one of my hidden talents." His voice was low, but vibrant with suppressed energy, husky with emotion. He stepped closer to her, bringing with him a clean, masculine scent and a radiating heat.

"And what's that?" Her mouth was dry and she felt as if she'd been plugged into an electrical outlet. She positively sizzled.

"In sixth grade I was voted the best kisser in the whole school." Without warning, he drew her into his arms and claimed her lips with his. For a single, fleeting moment Carolyn held herself rigid, knowing that to give in was to lose her mind. But mindlessness had a certain appeal, especially when it was Beau's lips making her so.

She moaned deep in her throat as his tongue slipped inside her mouth, stroking the hidden recesses with heated flicks. His hands on her back heated the cool silk of her gown as he pulled her closer against him, into the contours of his body.

Heady sensations assaulted her—softness and strength, silk and bare chest. She felt herself spinning out of control and welcomed it.

She groaned as his lips moved down the length of her neck, evoking fiery bursts of flame where they lingered. His breath was hot, his desire evident as he pulled her closer into the contours of his body. She ached with want, throbbed with need.

He slipped one of the shoulder straps of her nightgown down, then covered her bared breast with the palm of his hand. The low moan that escaped his lips only heightened her own desire. With a sigh of complete surrender, she melted fully against him.

Beau's senses reeled with the headiness of holding her close, caressing her silken skin, kissing her lips until they were swollen and pouty. He'd never wanted a woman as he wanted Carolyn. His body ached with his need to taste her, feel her, make love to her until they both fell apart, exhausted and fulfilled.

He dipped his head to the bud of her breast, touching it lightly with the tip of his tongue. She emitted a throaty gasp that only fed his hunger to possess her.

Desire battled with good sense. He wanted her but knew that making love to her would be the worst possible thing he could do. Things were unsettled between them. Hell, she wasn't even who she pretended to be. And she wanted to take his boys away from him. It was this final thought that cooled his ardor.

Gently, with a lover's touch, he reluctantly pulled the shoulder of her nightgown back in place. She looked up at him, her eyes glazed with passion, and his control momentarily wavered. "Go to bed," he said softly as he stepped away from her.

She tilted her head, as if disoriented. "Beau?" She reached out to him but he took another step back.

"We don't want to make a mistake." He smiled softly and reached up to touch her cheek. He allowed the caress to linger only a moment, then dropped his hand. "Just go to bed, Carolyn. We can talk in the morning."

She hesitated a moment, then nodded. Obediently she turned and went into her bedroom and closed the door behind her.

Beau leaned against the wall and drew in a deep breath, allowing his passion to dissipate slowly. He closed his eyes, trying to erase from his mind the burning memory of the taste of her lips, the sensation of her lithe body pressed intimately against his own. Running a hand across his lower jaw, he pushed him-

self away from the wall and went into his own bedroom. He got into bed and stared at the ceiling,
wondering what in the hell he was going to do about
Carolyn Baker.

Chapter Seven

He'd called her Carolyn.

It was the first thought she had when she opened her eyes the next morning. Now, she paced back and forth in front of her bedroom window, reluctant to leave her room and face Beau.

After their middle-of-the-night passion, the early-morning light seemed harsh, glaring, bringing with it a sanity that had been sadly lacking in the hallway the night before.

He could have taken her last night. He could have lowered her to the carpet in the hall and made love to her and she wouldn't have uttered a single word of protest. Rather, she would have aided him, encouraged him. She'd wanted it every bit as much as he had wanted it.

It shocked her, how easily he'd been able to delve beneath her defenses, make her feel things she'd never felt before. For the first time in her life, while in his arms, she'd felt a completeness that had been previously lacking, a surge of life that had been exhilarating.

And it shocked her that he apparently knew that she wasn't Carol Cook, nanny extraordinaire. What had given her away? How long had he known who she really was?

It was Sunday, her official day off. She didn't have to leave her room if she didn't want to. If the boys cried, she didn't have to be responsible for them today. But she wanted to be responsible for them today and every day. In the space of a mere couple of days they had crawled into her heart.

Much as Beau had. She frowned. Ridiculous. She wasn't about to fall in love with Beau Randolf. What she was experiencing was latent hormones kicking in, a physical reaction to a sexy, attractive man. It was nothing more than that.

She eyed the bedroom door and nervously ran a hand through her hair. She knew Beau was awake; she'd heard the shower in the bathroom running a few minutes earlier. Sooner or later she was going to have to face him.

"It might as well be sooner," she muttered. Taking a deep breath, she left her bedroom. She found Beau in the kitchen. He was clad in a pair of jeans and a T-shirt and sat at the kitchen table drinking a cup of coffee.

"Morning," he said as she entered. He gestured to the coffeepot. "Why don't you get a cup and join me?"

She nodded, trying to ignore how sexy he looked. His hair was slightly damp and tousled, and the dark gray T-shirt matched perfectly the color of his eyes.

Pouring a cup of coffee, she carried it to the table and sat across from him. She took a sip, her gaze not quite meeting his. "How long have you known?"

"Since the first night." To his credit he didn't pretend not to understand her question.

"What gave me away?"

He paused a moment and sipped from his mug. When he lowered it, an amused smile curved his lips. "This is a very small town, Carolyn, and mysterious deliveries from the local diner to this house were the talk of the town. How long did you think you could have dinner delivered and nobody would tell me?"

She shrugged, a flush of heat warming her face. She'd have preferred he didn't know about that particular ingredient in her duplicity. "I suppose you'll want me to pack up and leave as soon as possible."

"On the contrary."

She looked up at him in surprise. He gave her another amused smile. "I believe you owe me two weeks' notice. It will take me at least that long to find an acceptable replacement."

"You won't need one if I get custody of the kids."

The words hung between them for a long, awkward moment. Carolyn took a drink of her coffee, uncomfortably aware of his narrowed gaze on her. "You know I don't intend to give up easily," he said.

She nodded. "And I intend to use every weapon at my disposal to fight you."

His dark eyes caressed her boldly. "Is that what you were doing last night?"

Carolyn gasped, then compressed her lips tightly closed. "That was a low blow," she finally managed to say, her face hot with the memory of those moments shared in the darkened hallway. "And besides—" she lifted her chin and eyed him just as boldly "—I might accuse you of the same tactics."

He chuckled deeply. "Touché." His laughter died and he stared thoughtfully into his mug. "Carolyn, I want what's best for those kids—"

"And you think I don't?" she interrupted heatedly.

He sighed heavily. "No, I know your intentions are good. That's what makes it easy to forgive you for your little Carol Cook game, and that's what makes the whole thing so damned difficult." He sighed again. "I know you really believe you're doing what's best for the twins, but they don't need your money. I'm what they need. Casey's Corners is what they need."

"I disagree," Carolyn returned.

Beau held up his hands like a referee signaling timeout. "It's obvious this is a subject we won't agree on."

"And it's pointless for us to even discuss it. A judge will make the final decision," she continued.

He raked a hand through his hair, a frown cutting deeply into his forehead. "It's Sunday, your day off. As soon as the kids wake up, I'm going to take them to visit Iris. You're free to do whatever you want for the day."

Carolyn nodded, oddly deflated now that the cat was out of the bag and there was no glimmer of warmth or devilish desire in his eyes. Funny, for just a brief moment she felt a flare of jealousy—she was jealous of a woman named Carol Cook, a woman who, in reality, didn't exist.

She looked at him, wishing they could go back to the night before, back to the dance floor where he had held her close and made her laugh. Now an unpleasant tension radiated in the air between them. "Beau," she began, somehow wanting to dispel the tension. "It's nothing personal, you know."

He smiled tightly, his eyes as cold as a wintry day. "When somebody tries to take away something I love, I take it very personal. I guess I'm just funny that way."

As a cry came from the boys' room, he stood, his gaze still on her. "I don't give up easily, Carolyn, especially when I believe in what I'm doing. You won't find this an easy battle." Without waiting for her answer, he turned and left the kitchen.

Carolyn fought the impulse to run after him, knowing there was no way to change his mind, no way to make him see her side of this issue. They were at an impasse, at opposite ends of a pole; and the end result was that one of them would get what they wanted, and the other one would get hurt.

Within half an hour Beau and the boys were gone and the house resounded with silence. It was a silence Carolyn was familiar with, one of loneliness. Sometimes it seemed like she'd spent most of her life listening to it.

She went into her bedroom, deciding this was a perfect opportunity to make a dent in the mess. She threw away the boxes from the diner and put away the stack of sleepers and tiny T-shirts. It took her nearly an hour to completely clean and organize the room. Once finished, she went into the twins' room and sat down in the rocking chair.

It was a nice room. She wondered if the dinosaur wallpaper border had already been on the wall or if Beau had put it up since the twins had come to live with him. For some reason, the sight of the dancing dinosaurs made her sad.

She got up and found herself standing in the hallway just outside Beau's bedroom door. In the week that she'd been here, she'd never seen this, his most private space. The door was partially open, as if welcoming her inside.

She pushed the door wide and stepped inside, surprised to see that Beau Randolf apparently knew as little about housekeeping as she did. His bed was unmade; his bedside stand was littered with pieces of paper, coins, a coffee mug and a variety of miscellaneous items. The top of his dresser was just as chaotic, buried beneath magazines, clothing and cologne bottles. One thing was for sure: no matter who raised the twins, it was a certainty that whether it was Beau or herself, a housekeeper would be part of the equation.

The entire room smelled of Beau, the attractive blend of spice and fresh air and maleness. She knew the scent would be strongest in his bed, between the rumpled sheets where he slept and dreamed.

For a moment she entertained the impulse to slip into the untidy bed. Would she feel the same warmth as she had the night before when he'd held her in his arms?

The phone rang. She jumped guiltily, as if caught in the very act she'd just been fantasizing. She hurried out of the bedroom and into the kitchen, where she grabbed the receiver in the middle of the second ring.

"Hi, Carol."

"Regina," Carolyn replied as she recognized the friendly voice.

"I stopped by Iris's just a few minutes ago. I always bring her a fresh-baked coffee cake on Sunday mornings. Anyway—" she paused a moment to catch her breath, then continued "—Beau said it was your day off."

"It is." Carolyn barely managed to answer before Regina proceeded.

"Waylon just took the kids to the park, and I was wondering if you'd like to meet me someplace for lunch. You know, indulge in a little girl talk."

"I'd love to," Carolyn instantly agreed, grasping at the pleasant invitation to escape the quiet of the house.

"Great! Why don't we meet at Wanda's about eleven?"

"Is there any place else to have lunch?" Carolyn asked after a momentary hesitation. Not only was she fairly sick of Wanda's home cooking, but she was afraid she would walk into the café and everyone would giggle and point her out as the city woman who couldn't cook.

"There's the Bread Basket at the corner of Second and Oak. It has terrific salads and homemade bread."

"That sounds wonderful," Carolyn agreed. "I'll see you there at eleven." After hanging up, she decided to leave immediately. It was almost ten o'clock and she could wander up and down the sidewalks of Main Street and window-shop until it was time to meet Regina.

It was another unusually warm May day, with a slight breeze that smelled of summer. Carolyn walked slowly, enjoying the warmth of the sun on her back. She knew the first thing she was going to have to do was explain to Regina her real identity. She liked Regina, had enjoyed the woman's friendliness and vitality the night before. She didn't want to have lunch with her under false pretenses.

As she walked toward Main Street, people she recognized from the night before greeted her with cheerful hellos or friendly waves. Again Carolyn wondered if she would be making a mistake in taking the twins away from the coziness and friendliness of this small town.

But I can give them so much more than this, she thought. She couldn't have doubts now. She remembered her father telling her once that true strength was in making a decision, then sticking to it no matter how many doubts entered your mind. Carolyn had always considered herself strong and so she resolutely shoved aside any lingering doubts about gaining custody of the twins. She was doing the right thing, and she intended to follow through on her original plan.

At exactly eleven o'clock, she walked into the Bread Basket and immediately spotted Regina sitting at one of the tables near the window. Regina waved her over, a huge smile on her gamine face.

"Oh, this is so fun," Regina exclaimed when Carolyn was settled in the seat across from her. "I haven't had a chance to have lunch with a friend in a long time."

With a sigh, Carolyn immediately told Regina her real name and the reason she was in Casey's Corners. "When Beau mistook me for the housekeeper he'd hired, it just seemed a perfect opportunity," she finished.

Regina laughed, her brown eyes crinkling attractively at the corners. "We all were wondering why a woman who was a professional housekeeper would order her supper each night from the local diner. We also wondered how long you could afford to keep it up, but I guess for you that wasn't an issue."

Carolyn frowned. "Why do I feel like I need to apologize for my financial status?"

"Oh, hon, you shouldn't. It's just that I'm sure you live a life-style in New York very different from what we live here."

They stopped their discussion when the waitress appeared to take their orders. After she had departed once again, Regina looked back at Carolyn. "So, you're going to try to take the boys away from Beau?"

There was no censure in Regina's voice, no judgment at all, but Carolyn felt a flush warm her face. "I'm doing what I think is best for the twins," she defended.

"Oh, I'm sure you have their best interests at heart." Regina placed her napkin on her lap. "I just feel bad for Beau."

"I'm sure he'll adjust," Carolyn returned tightly. "Mary always told me Beau was the man about town. I'm sure he'll have no trouble finding some woman to soothe him."

Regina smiled. "Oh, yes, there was a time Beau was a devil with the women, but that was pretty much before Bob and Mary moved back here." She frowned thoughtfully. "I've known Beau since we were kids. He grew up in a wonderful family. His parents were loving, caring people. All the kids hung out at the Randolf house. Then suddenly his parents were gone and Beau was lost."

"And that's when he started spending time with Bob and Iris," Carolyn said.

"Exactly." Regina nodded. "Then Bob moved to New York and once again Beau was left adrift. That's when he started dating like a madman." Regina smiled, her affection for Beau apparent. "I think for the first time in his life, he felt truly alone, and it scared him. He settled down again once Mary and Bob moved back here. In all his wild dating, I think he was looking for something."

"What?"

Regina smiled. "He was looking for the place where he belonged."

Carolyn digested her words in shock. How was it possible that a wealthy woman from New York and a country man from Kansas could be seeking the same thing? It was a disconcerting thought: the idea that beneath the trappings, she and Beau shared a common desire, a common dream.

She was relieved when the waitress brought their orders and their talk turned to children. For the remainder of the meal Regina entertained Carolyn with stories of her four children.

It was after one o'clock when they reluctantly parted company. As Carolyn walked back to Beau's house, she thought of the lively Regina and how much she had missed having a close female friend in her life.

When she reached the house, Beau was carrying a plastic box out of the garage. The twins were already in their car seats and it was apparent he was getting ready to leave once again.

"Did you see my note?" she asked.

"Yes. Did you have a nice lunch?"

She nodded. "Regina seems like a really nice person."

"She's one of the best." He placed the box in the back seat of the car. "I was going to take the kids fishing. Want to come?"

"They fish?" she asked.

A small smile curved one corner of his mouth. "I fish. They drool."

"I'd like to come. I've never been fishing before," Carolyn said.

He pointed to the passenger door. "Let's go."

The ride was silent and strained. Carolyn didn't know what to say to him and longed for the easy relationship they'd had before the morning discussion. She wanted to see his eyes warm again, not the distant gray they were at the moment. She wanted to hear his laughter again, that wicked chuckle that always produced a responding smile in her.

"Where do you fish?" she asked, unable to stand the silence any longer.

"Randolf's Pond." Beau tightened his grip on the steering wheel, already regretting the impulse that had prompted him to invite her along.

"Randolf's Pond. Any relation?"

"It's on the place my parents used to own. When it was sold, the new owners promised me I'd always be welcome to fish the pond and it's a promise they have kept."

"Do you like to fish?"

"Sure. It's hard to hold on to stress with a fishing pole in your hand." He cast her a sideways look, noting how the sunshine streaming in the window danced on her dark hair and picked up fiery highlights of deep auburns.

He suddenly realized he was going to miss her when she was gone and those feelings were separate from the way he knew he would miss the twins. In the past week he'd spent his days at work looking forward to returning to the boys...and Carolyn. If she won the custody suit and she took the kids away from him, he would miss them desperately. What stunned and somehow angered him was to realize he was going to miss her, too.

Pulling his thoughts away from dangerous territory, he turned onto the dirt lane that led to the pond. Within moments it came into sight—a huge expanse of water that glistened in the sunlight. Beau instantly felt his inner tension ebb as he gazed at the peaceful pond with its surrounding woods.

"Oh, this is beautiful," Carolyn said softly.

"This has always been one of my most favorite spots. Almost every important event in my life has been celebrated, or cried over on these banks." He stopped the car and turned off the engine. For a moment he didn't move, but instead stared at the area and allowed old memories to play in his head. "When I was growing up, we had all my birthday parties right here. Mom and Dad cooked hamburgers out on a grill, then the kids would all swim or fish."

"You're lucky. You have wonderful memories of your family."

He turned and looked at her in surprise. "You don't?"

She shook her head, wistfulness shining from her eyes. "We didn't have time for birthday parties. Usually on my birthday the nanny would hand me a check from my parents." She looked away from him, out the window toward the pond. "My father was too busy running the corporation to plan a party or buy a gift and my mother, before her death, was usually off at some spa chasing the newest technique to keep her young-looking." She turned and looked back at him, her face slightly colored. "Sorry, I'm sure you don't want to hear about my distant past. Come on, let's go fishing."

Before Beau could reply she got out of the car and opened the back door to help with the kids. It took several minutes for them all to get situated on a large blanket by the end of the pond. The boys sat in the center, an array of toys before them.

Beau made a final trip to the car, carrying the last of the tackle, the bait and the fishing rods back to the blanket. He sat down on the edge closest to the pond and pulled the lid off the container of worms.

"What's that?" Carolyn asked, edging closer to him so she could see what he was doing.

"Bait." He looked at her, grinning at her squeamish expression as he pulled a worm out of the bedding. "I have an extra pole. You want to fish?"

She eyed him hesitantly, then watched him as he expertly baited his hook. "Will you fix it for me? You know, put the worm on?"

He shook his head. "Oh, no. If you're going to fish you need to bait your own hook. It's the only way to truly enjoy the whole fishing experience."

"Maybe I'll just watch you for a little while," she finally replied and sat down near him.

"Suit yourself." With an easy flick of his wrist, he cast the hook out into the water, then settled back in a prone position, his arms folded beneath his head and the rod and reel balanced between his knees.

He closed his eyes, lulled by the sounds of the kids' soft gibbering, the pleasant wind that stirred the tops of the trees and the sweet scent of Carolyn that permeated the air surrounding him.

"What happens now?"

Cracking an eyelid he saw that her attention was focused on the fishing pole, as if she expected it to spring to life at any moment. "We wait for the fish to bite."

"Oh. What do people do while they wait?" she asked curiously.

He sat up and smiled at her. "People do different things. Some sleep." He pointed to the twins, who had both fallen sound asleep. "Others think or meditate or talk. Tell me more about your family."

"You don't want to hear about that," she exclaimed.

"But I do," he protested. If she got custody of the boys, it was important that he know what kind of person she was, aside from her social standing and financial security. He needed to know that the kids really would be better off with her. "Did you ever think about doing anything else other than going into your family business?"

She shook her head. Again the wistfulness was back in her eyes. "At a very early age I discovered that the only thing my dad seemed to have time for was business." Again she looked away from him, focused on some distant point across the pond. "Business was the only thing he liked, the only thing he seemed to respect. I guess I figured the only way Dad would notice me, pay attention to me, was if he had to look at me every day at the corporation."

"Did it work?"

She smiled, but it was a sad little smile that touched Beau's heart. "Not really."

"Didn't Mary tell me you have a couple of sisters? Do they also work for the family corporation?"

"No." She was silent for a moment, obviously thoughtful. "We all coped differently with our parents' inattention. Bonnie—she's twenty-four, two

years younger than me—she coped by being outra-
geous. As far as Bonnie was concerned, negative attention was better than no attention." She smiled, as
if thoughts of Bonnie amused her. "She's in Europe
right now, probably destroying monarchies and causing chaos."

"And your other sister?" Beau asked, fascinated by
this peek into her personal life. Mary had spoken often of Carolyn, but hadn't told him very much about
her family.

"Colleen. She's the baby of the family, and she has
pretty well managed to carve a life for herself away
from the Baker name and business. She's a social
worker on Long Island."

"Whoa!" He jumped up as his fishing pole jolted
out from between his knees. Carolyn immediately
joined him, dancing with excitement as he reeled in the
line. "It's a real fighter," he exclaimed as the line first
zigged one way in the water, then reversed and zagged
in the other direction.

"Get it in," Carolyn said, her voice vibrating with
excitement.

Beau laughed. "I'm trying." He reeled faster, hoping he didn't lose it. "Wow, now that's a keeper." He
triumphantly pulled the fat catfish in and quickly
placed it on a stringer.

"Where's that other pole?" Carolyn asked.

He looked at her and grinned. "You ready to bait
your own hook?"

She returned his grin with one of her own and
pointed to Trent and Brent, who still slept peacefully.

"I figure if I can clean up their little bottoms, then I can handle a little bitty worm."

He popped open the container and held it out to her. As she withdrew a fat, wiggling worm, he had to admit to himself that at least she was a good sport.

Although he made her bait her own hook, he cast her line out into the water for her, then gave her the pole. "If you feel a tug on the line, then jerk the pole to set the hook," he instructed as he handed her the rod.

It took only a moment for her to get a bite. She jerked the pole so hard she lost her footing and tumbled backward, landing flat on her bottom in a patch of clover near the edge of the blanket.

Laughing, Beau held out his hand to help her up. "Are you all right?"

She nodded and grabbed his hand. As he pulled her up she stood directly in front of him. His laughter died as he remembered how it had felt the night before to hold her in his arms, taste the honeyed velvet of her lips. He wanted it again; wanted it so badly his body ached with the need.

He followed through on that need, pulling her against him as his lips sought hers. He didn't care whether it was right or wrong, smart or dumb. He only knew that holding Carolyn, kissing Carolyn, was what he wanted to do.

She responded with a hunger that surprised him, stirred his desire even higher. Her mouth opened beneath his, inviting him into a kiss of such depth, such intimacy, his head reeled with wonder. She smelled as fresh as the air that surrounded them, tasted as sweet as the patch of clover that enveloped them as they stumbled to the ground, still locked in an embrace.

There was no time for thought, no time for reason, there was only Carolyn and the magic of holding her, kissing her. She was like a fine wine, and with each sip he only grew more intoxicated.

Her mouth was hot, her tongue as aggressive as his, as the kiss lingered on. He felt himself responding with an intensity that stunned him. He was fire and she was oil, feeding the flames of desire higher and higher.

He could feel her heart, thundering in rhythm with his own as his hands moved beneath her blouse and caressed her breasts. The erotic feel of her lacy bra against the heat of her flesh only heightened his want. He felt the hardness of her nipples, pressing up as if seeking his caress, and a deep moan escaped his mouth.

He'd never wanted a woman as badly as he wanted Carolyn. He'd never felt such need, such want before in his life. Holding her in his arms filled an ache of emptiness he'd never realized existed deep inside him.

Carolyn was lost—lost in the sensations Beau evoked, lost in his scent, his feel, his very soul. As his lips moved down her neck, sparking heat where they touched, she yielded completely to him, wanting only the completeness his caresses promised would follow.

"Da-da."

The baby voice shattered the moment, brought reality slamming back to Carolyn's mind. Beau immediately sat up, a look of bewildered surprise on his face.

They both looked over to where Trent was on all fours, his baby face beaming a smile as he crawled toward them. "Da-da. Da-da."

Beau jumped to his feet, staring at the little boy in awe. "Did you hear that?" he asked Carolyn. "He said Da-da. He called me Da-da."

Carolyn stood up and straightened her blouse, embarrassment sweeping over her as violently, as intensely as desire had only moments before. "Yes, that's what it sounded like." She didn't have the heart to tell him she thought that Trent was just babbling and had no idea of the meaning behind the babbles. She didn't want to erase the look of wonder on Beau's face.

Beau reached out and plucked the crawling child from the edge of the blanket. "Hey slugger," he said. "Did you have a nice nap?"

Trent grabbed Beau's nose and laughed in glee. Despite the discomfort of the whole situation, Carolyn couldn't help but smile in response to Trent's antics. At that moment Brent woke up and, seeing his brother in Beau's arms, raised his hands toward Beau with a cry of outrage.

As Beau laughed and hefted Brent to his other hip, Carolyn's desire hit her square in the stomach once again. It wasn't a physical desire as much as it was the wish to be a part of a family, to be a part of something bigger than just herself.

As she watched Beau laughing and talking to the boys, she felt very much the outsider. Trent suddenly grinned at her and held out his hands, babbling as if trying to tell her something to make her laugh. He

bobbed up and down in Beau's grasp, then leaned toward Carolyn, his arms once again stretched out toward her.

"You'd better take him before he bounces right out
of my grip," Beau said. "Maybe we should call it a
day. These guys will be hungry before long," he said,
as Carolyn took Trent. "Besides, I'd like to stop by
Mary and Bob's and pick up some of the kids' things
on the way home."

"You don't have all their things?" Carolyn asked
curiously.

Beau shook his head. "Iris is the executor of Bob
and Mary's estate. When she took the boys, she took
what she needed to get by but left a lot of their things
at the house. Iris hasn't had a chance to take care of
much of anything concerning the estate, and as far as
I know, nobody has been in the house since the funeral."

It took them several minutes to pack up and reload
the car. As Beau drove back toward town, Carolyn
was grateful that he had no need to explain or discuss
their momentary lapse into insanity.

She didn't want to discuss, dwell on, even think
about those moments when she'd been in his arms. It
bothered her that it was getting more and more difficult to remember that he was her adversary.

Bob and Mary's home was a small, attractive ranch-
style. As Beau pulled into the driveway, a pang of
heartache clutched at Carolyn as she saw the flowers
that bloomed in the beds, the cheerful welcome wreath
that adorned the front door.

With Carolyn carrying Trent, and Beau toting Brent, they got out of the car and approached the house. Immediately upon entering, Carolyn knew her friend had been happy here. The decor radiated warmth and happiness.

"I'll just be a minute or two," Beau said, then disappeared down a hallway that led to the bedrooms.

Carolyn wandered through the living room, seeing signs of Mary's personality everywhere. Like Carolyn, Mary had been raised with wealthy, distant parents. Unlike Carolyn, Mary had been blessed in her marriage. It was obvious she had finally found love and a place where she belonged.

The kitchen only confirmed Carolyn's thoughts. Cheerful in tones of brilliant yellow, the room beamed with Mary's love of life. Carolyn paused in front of the refrigerator, where pictures of the boys and Bob were held by little magnets. Yes, Mary had been happy here. At least she had known happiness before her death. There was an odd piece of comfort in that.

Leaving the kitchen, Carolyn followed the hallway to the first bedroom, where Beau was packing a suitcase with little summer clothes. "I'm almost finished," he said.

"Take your time," Carolyn said as she moved to the next bedroom, apparently the one Bob and Mary had shared. Although the surfaces of all the furniture held a layer of dust, the rooms looked like they were just waiting for the couples' return. A book sat on the night table, along with a glass of water and a box of tissues. A pale blue nightgown lay across the foot of the bed. The sight caused grief to rise up inside Carolyn, and she backed out of the room, feeling like an intruder in an intimate setting where she didn't belong.

She backed into Beau and whirled around to face him, a tear slipping down her cheek. "You okay?" he asked softly.

She nodded and sighed tremulously, holding Trent tightly against her. "Mary was always after me to take some time off from work and come here to visit them. I wish—" She faltered and drew in a deep breath.

"I know." He reached out and caught her tear with his fingertip. "Let's get out of here."

Carolyn shook her head. "I want to see the rest of the house." She walked past him and poked her head into the bathroom. Conscious of Beau following her, she turned and smiled softly at him. "I know it sounds silly, but I want to see every room in the house. I want to be able to visualize Bob and Mary here . . . happy."

He nodded as if he understood and Carolyn moved on to the last bedroom, decorated in the universal style of a spare room. A single bed was covered with a floral spread, and a bookcase adorned one wall.

"I can't tell you how many nights I spent in this room," Beau said from the doorway as Carolyn walked over to the bookcase. She looked at the titles, unsurprised to find a selection of hardcover classics, mingling with paperback romances. Mary had always loved to read.

She turned and smiled at Beau. "She really loved it here, didn't she?"

He nodded. "I've never seen a woman more satisfied with her life and her choices than Mary."

"We can go now." Carolyn started to leave the room but hesitated as she saw a small dark maroon book and a handful of change on the top of the dresser. Frowning, her heart beating a curious rhythm in her chest, she walked over to the book and picked it up.

"Carolyn? What is it?"

Carolyn stared at the address book, her hand visibly shaking. "This . . . this is Sam's." She sank down on the edge of the bed, her head reeling in shock. "He was here . . . here in Casey's Corners, here in this house." She jumped back up, startling Brent who began to cry. "Sam was here. Oh, Beau, we've got to find him. He's in such terrible trouble."

Chapter Eight

Beau sat down next to Carolyn on the small bed. "Who is Sam?"

"He's my brother." She didn't look at Beau. She patted Trent absently with one hand. Her other hand tightly grasped the address book.

"I didn't even know you had a brother," Beau said in surprise. "Mary never mentioned him." Brent reached up and grabbed Beau's nose. Beau absently pulled his hand away.

"Sam is five years older than me. He wasn't around much when Mary and I were close." She raised eyes darkened with pain to Beau. "Sam has been missing for the last month." She stood once again. "Maybe he's been hiding out here, in this house, in this very room." Her eyes lit with hope.

Beau looked around the room, his law-enforcement training automatically kicking in. He looked back at Carolyn, knowing his next words would wipe the hope right out of her eyes. "Carolyn, look around. The dust in here hasn't been disturbed. Nobody has been in this room or in this house for several weeks."

His heart convulsed as her eyes once again lost the glow of hope and returned to a deeper, darker blue. "Are you sure the book is his?" he asked, once again removing Brent's little hand from his nose.

She nodded. "I gave it to him two years ago for his birthday. See, it has his initials right here." She traced a finger over the small gold letters.

"Come on, let's go home. Then you can tell me all about this missing brother of yours." He couldn't think with Trent crying and Brent wrenching his nose. And he had a feeling the story of Sam was going to take some deep thought.

The ride back to Beau's was silent apart from the twins' jabbering. Beau looked over at Carolyn, who still held tightly to the address book as if it was a lifeline to the missing brother. His blood throbbed as he smelled the brewing of a mystery.

When they got back home they fed the kids, then put them in their playpen. It wasn't until the boys were playing quietly that Beau took Carolyn by the hand and led her over to the sofa.

"Now, tell me all about this brother of yours and why he's missing," he said.

She stared thoughtfully at the kids, then finally turned and focused her gaze on Beau. "It all started with the murder of my father."

Beau sucked in a deep breath, and she closed her eyes, obviously fighting her emotions. He suppressed the urge to reach over and embrace her. He didn't trust that he could offer comfort without desire, especially remembering how quickly his passion had risen out by the pond.

"A month ago my father was murdered, shot in the head in his office at the corporation. It was late in the evening, the offices were closed. It was unusual for Father to even be there at that time." She hesitated a moment and picked up the address book from the coffee table. Her fingers gripped it so tightly, her knuckles turned white. "A witness saw Sam running from the building and the police have indicated that Sam is the prime suspect in the case."

"And what do you think?" he asked gently.

Her face reddened with rising emotion. "I think the whole idea that Sam had anything to do with my father's murder is absolutely ludicrous." She threw the address book back on the coffee table.

"So, where is Sam?"

Despair swept over her features. "I don't know. He disappeared on the night of the murder. He hasn't contacted me or my sisters. He hasn't been in touch with his wife or his little girl. It's like he vanished off the face of the earth. But this—" she pointed to the address book "—tells me he's been here in Casey's Corners. He might still be here somewhere."

"If he's innocent, then why is he hiding out?" Beau's mind was once again in the mode of a law-enforcement officer.

Carolyn frowned. "I don't know," she said again, her voice low and unsteady. "All I'm certain of is Sam's innocence." Tears sparkled on the ends of her lashes.

This time, Beau didn't fight his impulse. He placed an arm around her shoulders and drew her into an embrace. She burrowed her head against him and his heart responded to her on a purely emotional level.

As he held her his mind assessed what little she'd told him. The murder of a father, the disappearance of a son. He'd been involved in police work for too long to believe Carolyn's avowal of her brother's innocence unconditionally. People rarely believed family members were capable of heinous crimes.

"Tell me about Sam," he urged. She started to move out of his arms, but he tightened his embrace, unwilling to break the physical contact.

She sank back against him with a sigh. "I wasn't close to him when we were growing up. Sam joined the army when he was eighteen and spent the next ten years away from home. It wasn't until six years ago that he left the army and started working for the family business. Soon after that, he married Julianne and Emily was born."

"You're telling me what Sam has done, not what he's like," Beau objected. This time when she pushed to move out of his embrace, he reluctantly let her go.

She sat up and ran a hand through her hair, looking charmingly mussed and heartbreakingly vulnerable. "When he was growing up, what I remember most clearly about him was that he was an angry, rebellious young man." She smiled thoughtfully. "Sam always had a quick temper and he'd fight to the end for what he believed in, but when the argument was over he never held a grudge." The smile faded. "The arguments between Sam and my father were legendary around the offices, which probably didn't help Sam when the police began to look for suspects."

She looked at Beau, her eyes clear and determined. "All I can tell you is that in the past couple of years I got to know Sam better than ever, and he isn't the kind of man who would commit murder, especially the murder of his own father."

"So why is he running?" Beau pressed, his curiosity piqued.

"I don't know why, but I can tell you what I think." She hesitated a moment, obviously collecting her thoughts. "I think Sam was in the office that night and he saw something, maybe saw who the real murderer was, and now he's running for his life."

Beau slowly digested this information. "So, what would make him come here, to Casey's Corners?"

She frowned, the charming furrow appearing between her eyebrows. "The only thing I can think of is that Bob worked as head of security for Baker Enterprises for over a year. During that time Sam and Bob struck up a friendship."

"You think there's a possibility that Sam came here specifically to talk to Bob about something to do with the company?"

"I suppose it's possible," she agreed, "although it's also possible he just came here to hide out for a while. About a week before the car accident, Mary told me she thought she'd seen Sam here in town, but she wasn't sure. I didn't follow it up because we had people calling us every day to tell us Sam had been spotted first one place, then another."

"Maybe we need to ask around town, see if anyone else has had contact with him," Beau suggested.

"Oh, Beau, that's a wonderful idea." She stood, as if eager to get started right away. "Maybe he's still here somewhere, or somebody knows where he is."

"Wait a minute," he protested. He grabbed her hand and pulled her back down on the sofa. "Remember, it's Sunday. We'd be better off waiting until tomorrow morning to start asking questions when the businesses are open and people are back in their routines."

"I suppose you're right," she said reluctantly. She looked at the kids in their playpen and frowned.

Beau knew what she was thinking. It would be difficult for her to ask questions while toting the boys along. "I'll tell you what," he said, quickly making a decision. "I'll call Regina and see if she'll watch the twins for a couple of hours tomorrow, and I'll tell Waylon I'm taking those hours off. A lot of these people won't know you and might not answer your questions, but they'll talk to me."

She placed a hand on his arm and squeezed. "I don't know how to thank you."

Immediately he could think of several ways he would love for her to display her undying gratitude, but he wisely kept them to himself. Instead he stood. "I'll be right back. I'll go make that call."

When Beau left the room, Carolyn once again picked up the maroon address book and ran a finger over the gold initials. "Oh, Sam, what's going on?" she said softly.

She looked over at Trent and Brent, who were engrossed in a childish game of building towers with blocks. There had been a moment when they had all been out by the pond, when she'd entertained the thought of separating the kids. After all, it wasn't a case for King Solomon; there were two children, and two people fighting for custody.

She now dismissed that idea. Separating them to appease the wishes of two adults was no solution. Trent and Brent were brothers and deserved to be raised together, loving each other, supporting each other.

Perhaps if she and her sisters and Sam had been raised in a close, loving atmosphere, Sam wouldn't be missing now. He would be assured of his siblings' support and could face whatever charges had to be faced.

"All settled. We'll take the kids over to Regina and Waylon's around eight in the morning. She'll watch them for as long as we need her to," Beau said as he came back into the room.

Once again gratitude filled Carolyn's heart and she was relieved that she wouldn't have to face asking questions alone. "Now we have another major problem," she said.

"What's that?" Beau leaned down and picked up a block that Trent had tossed out of the playpen.

"If the diner is closed on Sunday nights, then what are we going to do for supper?"

He grinned—that wicked, sexy smile that made her heart flip-flop in her chest. "You don't cook at all?"

She shook her head and smiled sheepishly. "Not a thing."

"Then I guess we're at the mercy of my culinary skill for tonight. Come on, let's see what I can rustle up."

She followed him into the kitchen, thoughts of Sam on hold for the moment. Nothing more could be gained by wondering about Sam until morning when they could ask questions and hopefully get some answers. She sat down at the table and watched as Beau opened the refrigerator door and peered inside.

"Hmm, what are your feelings about eggs?" he asked.

She grinned. "I've always been glad that chickens are the ones who lay them."

His laughter warmed her heart, and she realized she didn't want to think about Sam or the custody battle. She didn't want to do anything but enjoy this moment of camaraderie between herself and Beau. "I've got cheese and mushrooms and fresh green onions. How about omelets?"

"Sounds good," she agreed. "What can I do to help?"

"Just sit there and stay out of my way." He gave her a supercilious grin. "As a master chef, I need plenty of room to create my masterpieces."

As he worked, she watched silently, admiring the efficiency of his motions, the familiar ease he exhibited. She also couldn't help but notice that the faded jeans he wore fit him to perfection, emphasizing his long legs and lean hips.

Occasionally she got up and peeked into the living room to make sure the boys were okay and happily occupied in the playpen.

"You like to cook," she observed as he eased the omelet out of the skillet and onto a plate.

"Yeah, I do," he said, as if surprised to recognize the fact himself. "I don't take the time to do it very often, but when I do, I enjoy it." He cut the omelet in half and slid one half onto another plate and set it before her. He made some toast, buttered it and added that to the table, then he poured them each a cup of coffee.

"It looks good," Carolyn said as he sat down across from her. "I'm sorry I never learned to do any cooking."

"It's never too late to learn a new skill," he replied. "I think it's particularly important for boys to know how to cook." He grinned. "So that they don't starve if they marry a woman who can't."

"I may not be able to cook, but I certainly know my fairy tales better than you," she teased.

He laughed and nodded, acknowledging her words. "You're right, but I figure at their age it doesn't matter much what I'm saying to them as long as I'm talking to them."

Again Carolyn felt a helpless inadequacy sweep over her. He seemed to know so much about what kids needed, what was important. What did she know about it? She had only her own dysfunctional background to draw from.

She focused on her food, chewing methodically as she thought. But I have love, she contradicted herself. I can give them so much, not only materially, but emotionally. She couldn't back down. Any day now a court date would be set and custody decided.

She suddenly realized with a jolt that somewhere in the space of the last couple of days the reason for her wanting custody had changed. She'd been telling herself for days that the reason she wanted custody was because they needed her. But it went deeper than that. No longer was it so much that they needed her; rather it was that she needed them.

"You suddenly got terribly quiet," Beau observed, breaking into her reverie.

She shrugged helplessly, unwilling to share her revelation with him. There was no reason to, it changed nothing between the two of them. "Just enjoying the delightful meal," she said, wanting to get back to the relaxed, uncomplicated mood of moments before.

"If you think this is delightful, you should taste my cornmeal-fried fish."

"If you hadn't let that catfish go, I could have tasted it," she replied.

"One catfish does not a meal make. We'll go back to the pond next Sunday and catch a whole mess of them, then have a real fish fry."

"And this time, when I feel a bite on the line, I won't fall backward and lose the catch," she vowed, then colored as she remembered what had happened between them after she'd fallen down.

His gray eyes lingered on her knowingly. "Maybe we need to talk about what happened this afternoon," he said as if reading her mind.

"There's nothing to talk about." Her face grew warmer and she knew it was probably turning a bright pink. His grin of lazy amusement only caused her cheeks to heat more.

"I believe there is. I think we need to talk about this obvious physical attraction thing you have for me," he answered.

"Me!" She gazed at him in outrage. "I don't have a physical attraction thing for you. Besides, as I recall, you initiated the whole thing, and you weren't exactly pushing me away with revulsion."

"I guess I have to confess I do feel a definite sexual attraction to you," he admitted, his smile widening.

"Despite my prunelike lips?" She glared at him. Now she remembered why she wanted custody of Trent and Brent. She didn't want them raised by this insufferable, obnoxious fool.

He laughed, his eyes warming her as they lingered on her mouth. "There's absolutely nothing wrong with your lips. In fact, I rather like them."

"Mary told me you were a difficult man to please when it came to women," Carolyn said, deciding to change the subject.

His laughter filled the room, seeming to brighten the dark corners. "Yes, that sounds like something Mary would say," he agreed. "She set me up on date after date, hoping somebody would click with me and end my bachelorhood."

"Mary wanted you to get married?" Carolyn asked.

Beau smiled softly. "Mary wanted everyone to be as blissfully happy and in love as she was."

"So, why haven't you gotten married?" Carolyn asked, shoving her empty plate away from her.

He stood up and started clearing the dishes. "That click that Mary kept hoping would happen, never has." He put their plates in the sink then turned back around to face her. He leaned back against the cabinets, a bemused expression on his handsome face. "Of course, that would be one way to solve our problem, wouldn't it?"

"What would?" she asked, not quite following him.

"Our getting married."

"That's a ridiculous idea," Carolyn scoffed unevenly. She stood and began to help clear the table, her heart pounding with an emotion that somehow frightened her.

"Of course, it's a ridiculous idea," he agreed, his voice gruff. "Why on earth would I want to marry a woman who can't even cook?"

"And why would I want to marry somebody who's arrogant, impossible and a slob?" Carolyn snatched up the last of the dishes and handed them to Beau.

"Well, at least we agree on this particular subject. We'd be fools to sacrifice our own happiness and futures to solve the problem." He turned to face the sink and twisted the faucets for water to start the dishes.

Carolyn sat down at the table and rubbed her forehead wearily. Naturally, he was right. They would be fools to contemplate marriage to each other to solve the dilemma of the custody of the kids. What she couldn't figure out was why, the moment he had mentioned it, had her heart soared? Why, for just a brief moment, had the thought of marrying Beau made her heart jump with something very close to joy?

Carolyn stood in the kitchen as the early-morning sun streaked the eastern sky. She shifted the phone receiver from one hand to the other and looked at her wristwatch. Almost seven o'clock. That meant it was nearly eight o'clock in New York. Surely Garrison would be in his office. She'd never known her father's partner to get to work later than seven-thirty.

"Garrison," she said at the sound of the deep familiar voice.

"Carolyn, is that you? Where are you, my dear?"

"I'm in a place called Casey's Corners, Kansas," she answered.

There was a pause. "When you told me you were taking off a couple of days, I figured you were taking a little vacation, but why on earth would you be vacationing in Kansas?"

Carolyn laughed. "It's a long story, Garrison." She sobered. "What I really called about was to find out how the investigation is going. Any news?"

"No, my dear, I'm afraid not." The older man's despair was evident in his tone. "Things in the investigation appear to have come to a halt. I still can't believe all this has happened. First Joseph's murder, then Sam's disappearance."

"I know, Garrison. So, there's been no word from Sam?"

"Nothing. I wish he'd just turn himself in so we could unmuddle all this mess."

"I know." She smiled at Beau as he walked into the kitchen. "Garrison, Sam has been here in Casey's Corners, might still be here someplace."

"What?"

Carolyn smiled her appreciation as Beau refilled her coffee cup. "I found his address book here, at a friend's house. We're going to ask some questions this morning and see what we can find out."

"Keep me informed. I'm worried sick about that boy."

"I will," Carolyn promised.

"And Carolyn... hurry home. The business needs you."

Saying goodbye, Carolyn hung up and joined Beau at the table. "That was Garrison Fielder. He was my father's best friend and partner." She wrapped her hands around the coffee mug. "I thought I'd better call him and see if he'd heard anything from Sam before we spend the morning asking questions."

"And?"

Carolyn shook her head. "Garrison has heard nothing, and the investigation into my father's murder is at a standstill."

"Do you have a picture of Sam?"

"Yes, as a matter of fact, I do." She jumped up and grabbed her purse from the counter. Pulling out her wallet, she quickly flipped through the photo section until she came to the one she sought.

She pulled it out of the plastic sleeve and stared at it for a long moment. The picture was of Sam, his wife and his little girl. The photo had been included in the

Christmas card Carolyn had received the previous year. She handed it to Beau.

He studied the picture for a long moment. "Nice-looking family," he observed.

Carolyn nodded and expelled a deep sigh. "Unfortunately, I don't think they'll ever be a family again." She leaned back in the chair. "It's funny. Sam is the only one of us who seemed to have it all together when it came to love and family. He and Julianne seemed to be so happy, but the last time I spoke to her she was so hurt and upset. Even if Sam surfaces and is vindicated, I don't know if he'll ever be able to pick up those particular pieces of his life."

She stared into her coffee, miserable as she thought of her brother and the family who loved him, but who might not be able to forgive and forget the past month of turmoil.

She looked up as Beau placed a hand on her arm. His smile was both sympathetic and supportive. "Finish your coffee, then let's go see what we can find out about this brother of yours."

Chapter Nine

"You two take a long as you need," Regina exclaimed as she walked Beau and Carolyn to her front door. "The boys and I will get along just fine."

"We really do appreciate it, Regina," Carolyn said, grasping Regina's hand warmly.

"Ah, get out of here." She gave Carolyn's hand a squeeze, then shoved her toward the door.

"So, where do we start?" Carolyn asked, the moment she and Beau were back in his car.

"Did you bring the picture?" he asked, easing the car out of the driveway.

She nodded and pulled her brother's photo out of her purse. "Beau, I can't thank you enough for taking the time to help me with this." Carolyn held the photo to her heart for a moment, hoping, praying that in the next couple of hours she would learn something about her brother's whereabouts.

"I thought we'd start on the east side of town and work our way down Main Street," Beau explained, maneuvering the car in that direction. "And you don't have to thank me. I'm a cop, Carolyn. This is what I do."

Carolyn studied his profile, for the first time realizing exactly what Beau did for a living. Funny, up until this moment she'd thought of him only in terms of the man who cared for the twins. She'd given very little thought to his professional life. "Is it dangerous? Being a deputy sheriff in Casey's Corners?"

He turned and gazed at her in open amusement. "Are you looking for reasons of unfitness to take to the judge for the custody hearing?"

"Not at all," she protested, irritated that he could take a genuine concern and twist it. "I have all the reasons I need to prove you're unfit."

His grin widened. "What, that I can't tell fairy tales?"

"That, among other things." She primly folded her hands in her lap and stared at him balefully.

"You can't say anything else. I have no other faults."

"And that, is one of your faults. You're arrogant," Carolyn returned.

He nodded his head. "That's true. I'm glad you noticed. I think a little arrogance is good for the soul."

"You must have a very healthy soul," she retorted, then sighed as he pulled into a parking space in front of the hardware store. "I just asked about the danger of your job because I was concerned."

He shut off the engine and unsnapped his seat belt, then twisted to face her. "Be careful, Ms. Baker." He reached out and traced the line of her jaw, his fingers feathers of fire against her skin. "Talk like that might make people think you actually care about me."

"Fat chance." She jerked away from his touch, unsnapped her seat belt and bolted out the door, her movements accompanied by Beau's devilish laughter.

He joined her on the sidewalk, his eyes still filled with mirth. "I can't help it, darlin', I just love to ruffle your feathers."

Carolyn wanted to hang on to her anger, needed it to battle Beau. But it was impossible to be angry, with his infectious grin softening his features. "You are impossible," she finally said as he opened the door to the hardware store.

"It's one of my charms," he replied.

However, the moment he approached the counter where an old man stood at the register, his charm disappeared beneath an aura of professionalism. "Charlie, can I ask you a few questions ?"

The old man's quizzical gaze shot to Carolyn, then back to Beau. "Is there a problem?" he asked.

"No. No problem. We're trying to locate a man named Sam Baker. Ever heard of him?"

Charlie frowned, pulling thoughtfully on the grizzled gray hair of one eyebrow. "Sam Baker? There are some Bakers that live out west of town, but I don't think any of them are a Sam."

Beau shook his head. "No, this would have been somebody new in town, somebody who just showed up within the last month." Beau looked at Carolyn, who pulled out the photo of Sam.

Charlie took the picture and studied it carefully. "Nope, never seen him before." He looked back at Beau, his blue eyes widened with a trace of excitement. "What's he done? Is he dangerous?"

"Absolutely not," Carolyn exclaimed, pausing as Beau placed a calming hand on her arm.

"Naw, we just need to ask him some questions. If you see him or know of anyone who has, let me know, Charlie."

"Will do," Charlie agreed.

As Beau and Carolyn left the hardware store, she tried to keep her disappointment under control. "You didn't really expect to hit pay dirt with the first person we spoke to, did you?" Beau asked, letting her know she hadn't hidden her emotions well at all.

She sighed and smiled. "Not really, but it would have been nice, wouldn't it?"

He placed an arm around her shoulders. "Darlin', you have a lot to learn about police work. Why do you think I'm so hardheaded?"

"I thought it was probably inherited. I just assumed you came from a long line of hardheaded men."

He laughed. "Nope, it's from spending so much time banging my head against dead ends."

After two hours of asking questions and flashing Sam's picture, Carolyn was feeling very hardheaded.

Nothing. Nobody seemed to have seen Sam or talked to him, or even heard his name before.

"Dammit, it's like chasing a phantom," Beau said in frustration as they left the florist shop. He paused on the sidewalk and looked at the few businesses left for them to check out. "How about we take a break and get some lunch?" He pointed toward Wanda's Café. "My treat, since you've bought me dinner a couple of nights."

She nodded, deciding to ignore his little gibe. They entered the café and Beau led her to a booth in the back. Once they were settled in, he reached across the table and took one of her hands in his. "Carolyn, you understand that if Sam was hiding out here, it's possible he didn't allow anyone to see him except Mary and Bob."

"I know," she answered, disentangling her hand from his as the waitress approached their table.

"Hi, Wanda," Beau greeted.

"Hey, Beau," the big woman beamed a pleasant smile to Beau, then to Carolyn. "And you must be my new favorite customer. The one who's been getting meals delivered?"

Carolyn smiled sheepishly. "I confess, I don't cook."

"That's all right, honey." Wanda winked in exaggerated camaraderie. "My mama always told me if you can't please them in the kitchen, then you damn straight better please them in the bedroom."

"You don't hear me complaining," Beau said as Carolyn gasped in outrage. He yelped as Carolyn's foot connected with his ankle beneath the table.

Wanda laughed and pulled an order pad from her pocket. "What can I get for you two?" She looked at Carolyn first.

"I'd like a chicken-salad sandwich and a glass of iced tea," Carolyn said as she envisioned Beau Randolf strangling on a chicken bone.

"And I'll take the burger special," Beau added.

The moment Wanda left the table, Carolyn glared at him. "What are you trying to do? Ruin my reputation?"

"On the contrary. If I wanted to ruin your reputation, I would have said you were bad in the bedroom." He pulled a couple of napkins from the container and offered her one. "Besides, what do you care what folks around here think of you? You won't be around for too much longer."

"That's true," she agreed, ignoring the curious pang that accompanied the thought of leaving Casey's Corners behind. She stared down at the tabletop, noticing that initials had been carved all over the wooden surface. She traced her fingers over T.D. + A.H. = True Love, wondering if T.D. and A.H. still lived here in Casey's Corners.

"It's kind of a tradition," Beau said.

She looked up and he nodded at the carvings. "Everyone who marries in Casey's Corners comes in here and carves their initials in one of Wanda's tabletops." He took her hand and guided her fingers to another carving.

"T.R. Loves S.G.," Carolyn said softly. "Who are they?"

"Thomas Randolf and Sara Greyson. My parents." He smiled. "Sometimes when I get lonely, I come to this table and just run my hands over the initials. It's my heritage, a link to this town." He pulled his hand away from hers. "Sounds stupid, doesn't it?" he said gruffly.

This time it was Carolyn who reached out and took his hand. "It doesn't sound stupid at all. I envy you that link, that heritage of love." She pulled her hand away as Wanda reappeared with their orders.

"My heritage is a carved tabletop and yours is a multimillion-dollar business," Beau observed when they had been served and Wanda had once again left the table.

"I've never considered Baker Enterprises my heritage," Carolyn disagreed. "For me it was always the vehicle to use to get closer to my father."

"And now he's gone."

She nodded. "And now for the first time in my life I realize that maybe I don't want to spend the rest of my life working for Baker Enterprises."

"What do you want?" Beau's gaze penetrated her, as if seeking some answer she didn't possess.

She looked down at the tabletop and her fingers found the carved outline of a heart. "I don't know," she replied softly, knowing only that she was confused.

They ate in silence. For some reason, their conversation had unsettled Carolyn, brought forward all her self-doubts. Garrison had told her to hurry home, that the business needed her. However, she knew that wasn't true. Baker Enterprises ran on well-oiled wheels with Garrison at the helm. It didn't matter whether she was there or not.

Again her thoughts turned to her father. Who could have killed him? What motive could somebody have had to kill him? According to the police, Sam's motive was business related. Sam had wanted the corporation to go public, and Joseph had fought the move. There was no way Carolyn would ever believe that her brother had anything to do with the death of her father.

She shoved her sandwich away half-eaten, one hand automatically going to the charm that hung on a gold chain around her neck. She fingered the charm thoughtfully.

"Not hungry?" Beau asked, pulling her from her thoughts.

"Not really." She frowned.

"Pretty necklace," he observed, leaning across the table to look closer. "Looks like it's some kind of bird."

She smiled. "It is. It's a phoenix. Father gave this to me the day before he was killed."

Beau reached across the table and took the golden bird in his hand, scrutinizing it more closely. "There's something written on the back?"

She nodded absently. "Some symbols. I think it must be the artist's signature." As he dropped the charm, she continued, "I just can't stop thinking about Sam. Surely if he was staying in Mary and Bob's spare room, Mary would have known about it. Why didn't she call me? Why didn't she let me know?"

Beau shrugged. "If Sam is in danger, as you believe, then perhaps he convinced her not to call you for some reason."

Anger warmed Carolyn's cheeks. "But if he's in danger that's all the more reason to contact us and let us know he's okay." She slapped a hand down on the table. "If nothing else, he should get in touch with his wife. This silence—it's so selfish."

Beau finished his hamburger and leaned back, a frown furrowing his forehead. "But if he's in danger, perhaps he's purposefully staying away from his family so as not to draw the danger to them. To me, that's not selfish. It's selfless and the greatest love a person can ever have."

"What do you mean?"

Beau shrugged again. "Maybe what Sam wants more than anything in the world is to be with his wife and child, but he is denying himself what he wants most for their best interests. That's real love—the kind that hurts to protect somebody else." He stood and threw a couple dollars on the table. "Come on, we've still got a few places left to check in this area before I head to the office."

As he paid Wanda for their meal, he asked her if she'd heard of anyone named Sam Baker. "Sam Baker? Nope, name doesn't ring a bell." She handed him his change, then took the picture Carolyn held out. "Yeah, I have seen him."

"When?" Beau asked, as a surge of excitement coursed through Carolyn.

Wanda frowned. "Couple of weeks ago. The day after Bob and Mary Johnson had their accident. He was standing out front that morning when I got here."

"Did he say anything? Did he say where he was staying?" Questions bubbled out of Carolyn.

"Nope, didn't say much at all. I got the impression he was headed out of town."

"What gave you that impression?" Beau asked.

Wanda shrugged her broad shoulders. "He ordered the biggest cup of coffee I had, and he was carrying a knapsack. When he left here, he headed out toward the highway."

"You sure it was him?" Beau asked, directing her attention back to the photo.

"Positive." Wanda flashed a broad smile. "Not too many handsome hunks come in this place. When they do, I notice."

"Thanks, Wanda." Beau handed Carolyn back her photo and together they left the café.

"He's gone, isn't he?" Carolyn said dispiritedly.

"I can't be sure, but I'd say if what Wanda told us is correct, he was heading out of town." He touched her arm, as if to comfort her. "We still have other places we can check out, see if anyone else saw him."

Carolyn shook her head. "No, it would probably be a waste of time. If Sam was still here, the best hiding place would be in Bob and Mary's house. It was obvious nobody had been there for a while." She smiled sadly at Beau. "He's gone, and we'd just be hitting our heads against those brick walls."

They got into the car and headed back to Regina's house. "I'm sorry, Carolyn. I wish we could have found him for you."

She shrugged. "Sam isn't going to be found until he wants to be found." She turned in the seat to face Beau. "I really appreciate all your help, Beau."

They rode in silence, Carolyn realizing it was time to put thoughts of Sam behind her for the moment. There was nothing she could do about her father's murder or Sam's disappearance. She could only help Sam if and when he wanted her help. In the meantime, she had to sort out her own life, which suddenly seemed filled with confusion and self-doubt.

"No luck, huh?" Regina asked when they got to her house. They had told her when they'd dropped off the kids that they were seeking leads to help them find Carolyn's brother.

"We think he left town a couple of weeks ago," Carolyn said, nuzzling Brent in her arms.

"Let's get the kids loaded up," Beau said, grabbing the diaper bags. "I told the guys I'd be in to the station around noon."

"Why don't you go on?" Regina suggested. "I can take Carolyn and the boys home." She shoved Beau toward the front door. "I don't get a chance for girl talk very often."

Beau looked at Carolyn. "Okay with you?"

"Sure, it's fine," Carolyn agreed.

"Then I'll see you later tonight." With that, Beau left Regina's.

"How about a cup of coffee before I take you home?" Regina asked.

"Sure," Carolyn replied, following her into the kitchen. Regina placed Trent on the floor and Carolyn did the same with Brent. The two kids immediately headed for the collection of plastic cooking utensils and bowls Regina had put out to amuse them.

"How do you keep everything so neat?" Carolyn marveled as she sat down at the table. She'd noticed that the living room was orderly and uncluttered, and the kitchen sparkled with cleanliness and smelled faintly of lemon cleaner.

Regina laughed and set a cup of coffee before Carolyn, then joined her at the table. "You just got lucky in coming here on a Monday morning. Monday is cleaning day. Come back on Wednesday or Thursday and you'll see bedlam."

"I have bedlam every day," Carolyn said dryly. "I can't seem to get the house cleaned and entertain the kids all in the space of one day."

"Welcome to the world of mothering."

Carolyn smiled. "When I decided to come out here and get the twins, I had the idea that mothering was easy, instinctive. It's been a rude awakening."

"Parenting is the toughest job anyone will ever do, but it's the most rewarding."

Carolyn smiled at Trent, who had a pink plastic bowl on his head. "I love them," she said softly.

"I know." Regina reached across the table and touched her hand lightly. "I guess there is one good point to all this. No matter who the judge decides to give the boys to, the kids will thrive. Either you or Beau will do a wonderful job parenting.'' She looked at the twins. ''They are very lucky little boys to have two people who care so much for them.''

''It all would be so much easier if Beau wasn't Beau.'' Carolyn paused to sip her coffee as Regina laughed.

''He is a charming devil, isn't he?''

''I wanted to hate him. I came out here believing that I would hate him. And there are moments when I want to positively wring his neck, but in the end, he makes me laugh.''

Regina took a drink of coffee, then studied Carolyn over the top of her mug. ''So, what are you going to do about it?''

Carolyn frowned. ''About what?''

''About the fact that you're in love with Beau.''

Shock riveted through Carolyn as heat filled her cheeks. ''I'm not... That's ridiculous....'' Unsteadily she set her cup down, trying to fight the wave of emotions that surged through her. ''I admit, I've grown very fond of Beau, and I admire the way he handles Trent and Brent. But, we come from different worlds. We both agreed that a marriage between us as a solution would be ridiculous. I have a life to go back to in New York. I'd be a fool to fall in love with Beau Randolf.''

Regina merely smiled. At that moment Trent cried, rubbing his eyes, and that started Brent crying. ''I'd better get you home. Looks like a couple of little pumpkins need a nap.''

Carolyn nodded, grateful for the interruption of what had become an uncomfortable conversation. As they packed up the kids and headed for Beau's, she told herself how ridiculous it was to even consider that she might be in love with Beau.

Minutes later, with Trent and Brent down for a nap, Carolyn wandered the house, going over and over her conversation with Regina in her head.

Regina was right about one thing. No matter how the judge chose in the custody suit, the ultimate winners would be the boys. Carolyn had no doubt that Beau loved the babies every bit as much as she did. But she wanted them. She wanted to see their smiling faces every morning. She wanted to tuck them in each night and kiss their baby sweetness. Was it so wrong for her to want to be the one who raised them? Was it so wrong to think that her financial position could make their lives better?

She jumped as she heard the familiar thunk of mail being deposited in the slot by the front door. She grabbed the envelopes, intent on placing them on the kitchen counter, as she did every day.

As she walked through the living room, her gaze was captured by the top piece of mail, and the official seal that adorned the return-address spot. It was from the courthouse and she knew it probably held the information about the date of the custody trial.

Her hand trembled as she set the envelopes on the counter. She would have to wait until Beau opened it to find out how much longer she would be here in Casey's Corners.

She sank down at the table, overwhelmed as she realized she'd lied to Regina. She'd managed to do something incredibly stupid. She'd fallen in love with Beau Randolf.

Chapter Ten

"Dammit, Waylon. I've told you again and again not to put the arrest forms in this file." Beau slammed the metal cabinet and turned to glare at the overweight deputy.

"Sorry, Beau." Waylon shifted uncomfortably in his wooden chair.

Beau swiped a hand through his hair, then stared at his friend. "No, I'm sorry. I didn't mean to yell at you." He sank down on the chair behind his desk and once again raked a hand through his hair. "It's this custody suit. It's making me crazy."

"Next Wednesday, right?"

Beau nodded. Five more days and the fate of the twins would be decided. Since the moment the letter had come four days before from the court informing him of the date, he and Carolyn had walked on eggshells with each other. Both were suddenly aware that within days, their lives would irrevocably change. Beau expelled a deep sigh. "It's crazy. I don't know whether I'm scared I will get custody or scared that I won't."

Waylon looked at him in surprise. "What are you talking about? You changing your mind about what's best for those boys?"

Beau grinned wryly. "Only every other minute." He tipped the chair up on its rear legs and leaned the back against the wall behind him. "Most of the time I know I can give those boys everything they need to grow up to be well-adjusted, productive adults. I love them more than anything or anyone I've ever loved in my life." He flushed, unaccustomed to speaking of his feelings so freely.

"So why the doubts?" Waylon asked.

Again he raked a hand through his hair. "There are moments when I wonder if maybe I'm depriving them of a much better life-style. There's no getting around it, Waylon, Carolyn can give them things I can't afford."

"Yeah, but can she love them like you do?"

Waylon's words haunted Beau for the rest of the day. In truth, Beau didn't know how capable Carolyn was of giving love. She, herself, admitted she was the product of distant, uncaring parents. How could she give what she'd never had herself?

He didn't doubt the fact that Carolyn loved Trent and Brent as best she could, but was it enough?

These questions plagued him as he drove home and they followed him into the house, where the scent of tomato sauce was redolent in the air. "Carolyn?"

"In here," her voice drifted out from the kitchen. He stumbled over a plastic dump truck and kicked a ball from his path. As he entered the kitchen, Trent and Brent immediately crawled toward him.

"Hey, little rug rats."

Carolyn turned from the stove, her glasses fogged with the steam rising from a pot of boiling water. "This will be ready in just a minute," she said, then smiled proudly. "I'm cooking."

"So I see." He walked over to her and gently removed the steamed glasses, noting the attractive flush in her cheeks. He placed the glasses on the counter next to where she worked. "What exactly are you making?"

She held up a handful of spaghetti and dropped it into the pot. "I have to confess, I cheated on the sauce. It's jarred from the store, but it's a start."

"Yes, it is." He moved away from her, irritation winging through him. Next thing he knew, she'd be entering the Mother of the Year contest.

He sank down at the kitchen table, smiling as Brent crawled over to him and pulled himself up to a standing position, using Beau's knees for support. "Hey, little man, have you been good today?" Trent quickly joined his brother, competing for Beau's attention by jumping up and down and squealing with excitement. Beau laughed, finding it difficult to hang on to his foul mood with the kids' entertainment.

He looked up to see Carolyn watching him. He motioned to the pot. "You might want to stir that spaghetti, otherwise it tends to stick together."

She turned quickly, doing as he'd suggested. He noted how her hair shone in the waning evening sunlight that filtered in through the windows, then admired the snug fit of her jeans across her shapely derriere. "You're wearing jeans," he said in surprise.

Facing him once again, she smiled self-consciously. "I took the boys shopping today and bought them. Today seems to be the day for firsts—jeans and cooking."

"Careful, or your friends won't recognize you when you go back home."

Her smile quickly faded and she redirected her attention to the boiling pasta. Beau's irritation returned, unbidden and unwanted, but impossible to ignore. He played with the boys until she drained the spaghetti, then he stood. "Is there something I can do to help?"

"You can get the salad out of the refrigerator," she said as she placed the spaghetti in a bowl and added the sauce over the top.

He took out the salad, then placed the boys in their high chairs. By that time she had the spaghetti on the table, along with a loaf of hot, crispy garlic bread.

Supper was silent, the same tension evident that had been present since the arrival of the letter from the court. When Brent dropped his spoon, both Beau and Carolyn reached for it, bumping heads in the process.

"Sorry," Carolyn murmured. She sat back up, feeling like an eruption was imminent between them.

In the past couple of days, she'd tried to withdraw mentally and emotionally from Beau, needing to distance herself both for the court fight to come and for leaving Casey's Corners and Beau behind.

The realization that she loved him had only managed to twist her heart more desperately and heighten her tension when he was around. She'd like to think he was in love with her, but she knew better. He'd admitted to a certain physical attraction, but that was a long way from the love and commitment Carolyn had come to yearn for in her life.

He'd made it clear he would fight her to the end for custody. How many of his kisses had been a form of subtle manipulation? A shrewd attempt to soften her up and get her to change her mind about seeking custody of the twins?

Since the letter had come and the date had been set, Beau had also withdrawn. There had been no more soft glances, no more sweet kisses, no more jokes or camaraderie. Maybe she would have been better off not knowing the fullness of love, because she'd never realized before how much love could hurt.

After supper, they worked together to clear the table, falling into the easy routine they'd established when she'd first arrived.

It wasn't until the kids were in bed for the night that Carolyn decided to try to ease the strain that had been a constant barrier between her and Beau.

She sat down next to him on the sofa, where he was reading the evening paper. "Beau, we need to talk."

"Talk about what?" He didn't lower the paper.

"About the custody suit."

"What about it?"

Carolyn stared at the paper in frustration. How could she have a serious talk with him through newsprint? "Beau, would you please put the paper down?"

He folded it with meticulous care, then looked at her expectantly. His gaze was cold and distant, as it had been for the past couple of days.

"Beau, I don't want us to be enemies. No matter how the judge decides in this matter, I'd like to think we can still be friends."

"Sure, we can remain friends. You can write the boys here as often as you like."

Carolyn flushed. "You're so certain you're going to win?"

He studied her thoughtfully. "Tell me again why you want custody, Carolyn."

"Because they need me." She raised her chin. "I can give them things you can't."

"The same kinds of things your parents gave you?"

"I won't make the same mistakes my parents did. I know what was missing in my childhood, and I'll make certain Trent and Brent have those things." She leaned forward and placed a hand on his arm. "Beau, I know I have a lot to learn, but I'd be a good mother." She wasn't sure why it was so important that he believe in her abilities to be a good parent, but it was important to her. "I love them, Beau," she finished.

"I know you do." He sat forward and raked a hand through his hair. "I'm just not convinced your love is the kind they need."

"What does that mean?" Carolyn glared at him, her anger stirred.

He shrugged. "The experts say dysfunction is handed down from generation to generation. No matter how much you say you won't make the same mistakes as your parents, the odds are not in your favor."

Carolyn stood her anger causing her to tremble. "You're so self-righteous, so certain in your belief that your love is the only kind that is good and pure. Consider this, Mr. Perfect. If you get the boys, then you can have a family without making a real commitment to a woman. You can have your family and still date your big-breasted bimbos at the same time."

"And you consider this." He also stood, his face a thunderstorm in the making. "You can tell yourself all you want that those kids need you, but that's not the case. They don't need you. You need them. You need them to make your life count for something. You've lived your entire life being a wealthy Baker corporation. They're your chance to be a real woman."

For a moment they continued to glare at each other, the tension fully erupted into waves of frustration and anger. The ringing of the phone split the momentary silence.

Beau stalked off to the kitchen to answer it. He returned a moment later. "I've got to go. There's been a break-in at the Lambert house." Without waiting for a reply, he bolted out the front door and into the night.

The slam of the door elicited an immediate response from Trent and Brent's bedroom. They wailed.

"Thanks a lot,"Carolyn muttered, hurrying in to soothe the kids.

Beau sighed tiredly as he headed home. It was well past midnight, he was exhausted, and the memory of his fight with Carolyn weighed heavily on his mind. He'd struck out at her, intentionally wanting to inflict hurt.

But her words had stung him, surprised him with their insight. Oh, he had no interest in dating a string of big-breasted bimbos, but he wondered if perhaps she hadn't been right in her assessment that he wanted the kids to provide him a family without commitment.

Mary had often accused him of being commitment wary, of subconsciously choosing inappropriate women to date so he didn't get emotionally involved with them.

He admitted to himself now that he was afraid of marriage, afraid of commitment. He wanted so badly to have the kind of marriage his parents had, the kind Mary and Bob had, and was afraid of making a mistake.

Still, he wanted somebody special in his life; somebody to whom he could tell his dreams, somebody to hold in the night, to share the laughter and tears of life. Somebody like Carolyn.

He pulled into the driveway and stared at the darkened house, shocked by his thoughts of Carolyn. Ridiculous, it was utterly ridiculous to consider a lifetime with her. She had a business to run, a life of her own in New York, and her life-style sure as hell didn't include a hayseed deputy with an attitude problem.

He got out of the car, exhausted both physically and mentally. As he entered the house he immediately smelled Carolyn's sweet scent. It lingered in the air like the remaining echo of a pleasant song. He wondered how many days it would take after she left before her scent would be gone?

Entering the kitchen, he saw the remnants of cookie crumbs on the high-chair trays. Evidence that the kids had been awake while he'd been gone. He grabbed the container of juice out of the refrigerator and popped the top off. Taking a long, deep swallow, he remembered Carolyn yelling at him about his manners, and realized again that he would miss her when she was gone.

Scowling, he put the juice back in the refrigerator and left the kitchen. As always, before heading to his own room, he went into the twins', wanting a look at their sleeping faces before drifting into his own dreams.

He leaned over the first crib and the blood left his face. Empty. The crib was empty. He raced to the other bed. A pile full of blankets and a stray moonbeam. No baby.

Had the fight they'd had earlier prompted Carolyn to take the kids and run? Anger blasted through him, along with a riveting sense of betrayal. Had she just assumed that her money elevated her above the law? Damn her wealthy hide.

He left the kids' room and stalked into her bedroom. He threw open the door and froze on the threshold. There, on the bed was Carolyn, clad in her sexy blue nightgown and babies. She was sound asleep, a slumbering child on either side of her. One of Trent's hands was tangled in her hair, and Brent's chubby baby fingers rested on her cheek.

Shame replaced his anger. Guilt usurped his feeling of betrayal. He should have known she wouldn't steal the kids and run away.

She'd placed a chair next to the side of the bed, providing a barrier should Trent roll away from her. His heart convulsed as he slowly accepted the fact he'd tried so hard to deny: Carolyn would make a wonderful mother.

Carolyn sat next to the bathtub, watching the boys splash and play in the water. She captured every one of their facial expressions, intent on keeping the memory in her heart where she could pull them out and remember them at will.

Beau was working late and had told her he probably would be home just in time to tuck the kids in and tell them their bedtime story. She intended to have them ready, freshly bathed and smelling sweet.

In the past two days, since the night of their fight, Carolyn had scarcely seen Beau. He'd gone to work early and stayed late every day, as if unable to be in the same house with her for any length of time.

And in the time Carolyn had alone, she'd come to a decision. The most painful decision she'd ever made. She felt the sting of tears burning hot behind her eyelids and consciously willed them away.

"Ba-ba-ba." Trent slapped his hands against the surface of the water and squealed in delight as the resulting splash hit Carolyn.

"Okay, you little fish, time to dry out." She lifted Trent from the water and wrapped him in a big fluffy towel, then set him on the floor and repeated the process with his brother. "Come back here, you!" She chased after Trent, who had abandoned the towel, his bare bottom wiggling as he crawled out of the bathroom.

She scooped him up and nuzzled his neck, the resounding giggles causing tears to once again press at her eyes. Scurrying back into the bathroom, she grabbed Brent and carried them both into their bedroom where she deposited each in his own bed.

As she wrestled Trent into his diaper and sleeper, Brent bounced up and down, grinning and chattering like a little magpie.

Beau had been right. The boys didn't need her. She needed them. She'd wanted them to fill the empty spaces in her life, chase away a lifetime of loneliness. And that was heavy responsibility to lay on the heads of two little boys.

While she dressed Brent, her mind replayed the conversation she'd had with Beau on the day they had searched for Sam. She'd claimed Sam was being selfish. But, Beau had suggested that Sam might be being selfless, putting his family's safety above his own wants and needs.

"Looks like I'm just in time."

She whirled around to see Beau standing in the doorway. "Yes, they're all ready for bed," she said as she finished snapping Brent's sleeper. "They were just telling me how anxious they are for their bedtime story."

As he sat down in the rocking chair, she kissed Brent's head, inhaling deeply of the sweet, baby scent. She moved to Trent's crib and did the same. "I think I'll go ahead and go to bed, too." Without waiting for Beau's reply, she left the bedroom and went into her own.

She waited several minutes, then grabbed the handle of her suitcase and cracked open her door. Stealthily, like a thief in the night, she crept out of her room and closed her door. She paused momentarily in the hallway just outside the kids' room.

The creaking of the rocker mingled with the deep sounds of Beau's voice. "And then, Hansel and Gretel planted the beans and a huge beanstalk sprouted up to the sky."

She leaned against the wall and stifled a combination of a sob and a giggle. How could anyone confuse Hansel and Gretel with Jack? She closed her eyes, fighting to sort out the difference between what she knew she must do and what her heart wanted her to do.

She wanted to stay here, wanted to be a part of Trent and Brent's future. Worse, she wanted to stay here and be a part of Beau's future. She knew she couldn't stay here another day, another minute, and not tell him how much she loved him. The emotion she felt was too much to hold inside any longer.

Loving Beau was the last thing she'd expected to happen, and she knew her heart would forever bear the scar of that love. She also knew his feelings for her. He'd made them clear when they'd had their last argument. He thought she was incapable of loving, believed she was nothing more than a wealthy bum looking for a new toy.

Well, he was wrong about one thing. She loved those kids more than she'd ever dreamed possible—enough to know he was the best parent for them, enough to walk away from them.

Goodbye, she mouthed silently. Tears falling freely, Carolyn picked up her suitcase and quietly left the hallway. She headed for the front door, pausing only long enough to place a letter she'd written on the coffee table. Then, saying another silent goodbye to the man and boys who had stolen her heart, she left.

Chapter Eleven

Beau awoke to the cries of the twins. He frowned and reached for his alarm clock. A few minutes after six. He lay still for a moment, waiting to hear the sounds that would indicate Carolyn was up and tending to the boys.

When the crying continued unabated, he roused himself from the bed. Yanking on a pair of jeans, he hurried in to the kids, who were wet and hungry and eager to face a new day.

"Okay, gang," he said, grabbing a couple of fresh diapers from the diaper bag. Where was Carolyn? Surely she could hear the twins raising the roof.

He wrestled Brent down for a diaper change. "I guess your mama decided to take the morning off," Beau muttered, then bit his tongue at his Freudian slip. Funny, how in his mind he thought of Carolyn as the boys' mother and of himself as their father. Since she'd arrived, there had been a sense of family in the house that had been absent before.

He shook his head to dislodge these thoughts. Moving from Brent to Trent, he finished the diapering job, then swung both kids into his arms and carried them out to the kitchen. He planted them in their high chairs, gave them each a cracker, then set about making coffee.

As the minutes ticked by, he was surprised that Carolyn didn't make an appearance. She usually beat him out of bed in the mornings, insisting she needed to get a jump on the day before the twins awakened.

She'd gone to bed early the night before, and as far as he knew, the kids had slept through for a change. So, why wasn't she awake? Why wasn't she in here sharing her first cup of coffee with him?

He poured himself some coffee and walked to the front door. He pulled it open, allowing the fresh-scented morning air to waft through the screen door. He sipped from his cup, then froze as he realized there was an unusual space by the curb in front of his place. Carolyn's rental car was gone.

Setting his cup down on the coffee table, he raced from the living room to her bedroom. Opening the door, he stared around, his heart thudding dully as he saw the emptiness of the room. She was gone. The only thing left was the lingering scent of her perfume.

He turned and left the room, confusion muddling his thoughts. Why had she gone? Where could she be? What in the hell was going on in her head?

Then he spied the note with his name written boldly at the top. He picked it up and read. When he finished, he set the note aside and went back into the kitchen, trying to sort out the tangle of his emotions.

She was dropping her suit. She wouldn't fight him for custody of Brent and Trent. She'd given no explanation or reason for her change of heart.

He should be flying high with happiness. The fight was over and he had won. Looking at the kids, he waited for the elation to hit, waited for triumph to soar through him. It didn't come.

All he felt was a dull emptiness, and the overwhelming feeling that he'd made a tragic mistake. "Ma-ma," Trent said, then grinned at Beau and slobbered a trail of cracker crumbs.

"Yeah." Beau eyed the two boys soberly and realized he'd won the war, but he'd allowed the coveted prize to slip away. He'd allowed his own fear of making a mistake to blind him to the fact that he was in love with Carolyn Baker.

But what did he have to offer her? A two-story house that needed a paint job, a small-town existence in the middle of Kansas. When compared to her luxury life-style in New York, it came up hopelessly short.

Still, didn't he owe it to himself to let her know at least that he loved her? He looked at the twins again. Didn't he owe it to them to put his pride on the line and bare his heart, his soul to her? If she turned him down, told him she didn't love him, then at least he'd know he'd tried.

"Ma-ma-ma-ma," Brent chanted, as if reading Beau's thoughts.

Beau stood and grabbed each of the boys. "We're going to go find your mama right now."

Carolyn awoke to sunshine streaming in the window. She rolled over, still half-asleep, and gazed at the clock on the bedside stand. Almost ten o'clock. Ten o'clock! She sat up, one leg seeking the floor, then remembered there were no Trent and Brent waiting for her to get them out of bed. She would not have her first cup of coffee with Beau's gray eyes mischievously caressing her over the rim of his cup.

She flopped back down, staring up at the cracked motel-room ceiling. She'd driven an hour away from Casey's Corners before stopping and getting a room. Her eyes felt gritty from lack of sleep and too many tears.

"It was the right thing to do," she whispered to herself. Giving up her fight for the boys had been the single most difficult, and the single most right thing she'd ever done.

Beau was a natural parent; his love for the boys came as naturally as breathing. She'd had to struggle with every aspect. She hadn't been able to keep the house organized, she couldn't cook worth a darn and she had never managed to glow because of her mothering.

Yes, she'd done the right thing, but that knowledge didn't make it hurt any less. The pain was twofold. Leaving the boys behind and knowing she would never be an active part of their lives was difficult. Leaving Beau behind and knowing her love for him would never be reciprocated was devastating.

She got out of bed and stumbled to the bathroom, grateful that she didn't have her glasses on. She had a feeling the room would only be more depressing if brought into clear focus. She hadn't much cared last night where she stopped, needing only the solitude of a private place to cry.

After showering, she dressed in a pair of slacks and a floral blouse. Travel clothes. She had another hour-long car drive, then a plane ride ahead of her. Back to New York.

She had made a decision in the middle of her tears the night before. She would not be returning to her position at Baker Enterprises. In the past couple of weeks with Beau, Carolyn had realized how empty her life was in New York. A change was in order. She didn't know what kind of changes would be made, only that she needed to find something for herself outside her family name and corporation.

Brushing her hair in front of the warped motel-room mirror, she carefully kept her thoughts schooled away from Beau. She didn't want to think about his bold, bedroom eyes or charming smile. She didn't want to think about the sweetness of his kisses or the heat of his caresses. It hurt.

A knock sounded on the door. Carolyn whirled around in surprise. She checked to make certain the security chain was in place before easing the door open a crack. "Yes?"

"Highway patrol, ma'am. Would you open the door?"

She stared in surprise at the blue uniform of the officer. "Wha-what's going on?"

"I'd like to ask you a few questions."

Carolyn stared at him for another full minute. Was she in trouble? Had she done something wrong? She could see the patrol car behind the officer and slid the security chain off.

As she opened the door, the officer stepped aside and Beau walked in, the boys riding his hips on either side. "Thanks, Greg, I owe you one," he said.

"I'll remember that, Randolf." Greg grinned widely, then strolled back to his car.

"What are you doing here?" Carolyn asked, trying to ignore the delighted grins of the two boys, the amused smile on Beau's face, and the heavy pounding of her own heart.

He walked over to the bed and deposited the kids in the center of the mussed covers. He dumped a small knapsack full of toys between them, then turned back to look at her. "We need to talk."

"How did you find me?" she asked, wrapping her arms around herself to stave off the desire to touch him, rush into his arms.

"I put out an unofficial all-points bulletin on a description of your rental car. Greg spotted you here and gave me a call."

"I can't imagine why you went to all the trouble," she returned unevenly. "We have nothing to talk about."

"I think we do." He moved closer to her. "We made a deal that you would stay and take care of the kids until the custody hearing. It's still two days away."

"So, sue me." She took a step backward. Damn him, was that what worried him? He didn't have a baby-sitter for the next two days?

"Why did you leave before the court date?" He took another step toward her and she backed up, bumping against the wall.

"Because there was no point in staying," she replied angrily, tears burning hotly as they fell from her eyes. She swiped at them impatiently. "You won, Beau. I give up. Just go and have a nice life."

His arms reached out on either side of her, his hands bracing him and effectively capturing her. "Why did you decide to drop the suit?" His gaze bore into hers, intent and direct.

"What difference does it make?" She wanted him to move away from her, couldn't stand the heart-break of his closeness. Why was he tormenting her? Couldn't he see that his nearness alone had her trembling?

"I need to know, Carolyn. What made you decide to drop the suit?" His voice was tense, strained, but his eyes gave away nothing of what was going on in his head.

She leaned her head back against the wall and closed her eyes. "Because you were right." She opened her eyes and looked at him. "You would make a better parent to them." Tears burned once again and she swallowed hard. "I love them enough to do what's right, and you're the right one to raise them."

"How can you say that?" He glared at her incredulously. "You know I'm arrogant. You know I'm a slob and have no manners."

"Yes, but I don't cook and I can't even keep the house clean."

"How can you think about leaving those poor little tykes alone with me? You know I can't keep my fairy tales straight. I thought you loved them."

"I do love them," Carolyn protested.

He leaned into her, so close his breath caressed her face. "Then don't leave them," he whispered.

She tried to evade him, needing to distance herself, unable to think with him so close. She managed to duck under one of his arms and stepped toward the center of the room. "What are you talking about?" she asked breathlessly.

He raked a hand through his hair, causing it to stand on end. "Just what I said.... Don't leave them.... Don't leave me."

Carolyn's heart seemed to skip a beat, then pounded with such ferocity it echoed in her ears. "What are you saying?" She looked over at the boys, happily involved in playing with the toys, unaware of the human drama playing out. "Are you suggesting I stay here and continue being the nanny? The housekeeper?"

"No, I'm talking about you staying here and being the twins' mother." With long strides he reached her, his hands gently grasping her shoulders. "I'm talking about you staying here and becoming my wife."

She shrugged his hands off her shoulders, a flush warming her cheeks. "What? An arranged marriage, a matter of convenience? I couldn't do that, Beau...I—" She broke off, appalled that she'd almost bared her heart, that she'd almost told him she loved him.

He leaned against the dresser and smiled the devilish grin she loved so well. "Let me tell you what I want, darlin'. I want a marriage like my mama and daddy had, one like Bob and Mary shared. I want to spend the rest of my life with a petite, nearsighted, noncooking woman." The naughty smile fell from his lips, replaced by a hunger, an intensity that stole Carolyn's breath away. "I love you, Carolyn Baker. I don't want to raise these kids alone. I want to do it with you."

She inhaled sharply, unable to move, unable to do anything but stare at him. "I . . . I . . ."

He shoved away from the dresser and reached for her, pulling her into his arms. He looked down at her, his eyes radiating his fear. "You what?" he asked urgently.

"I . . . I love you, too." Her words escaped her with a burst of laughter as he picked her up off the floor and swung her around.

"Really?" He stopped moving and brushed a strand of her hair away from her eyes. "You really love me?"

She laughed and nodded her head. "I really do."

He sobered, his gaze connecting with hers in a way that caused her to shiver in delicious anticipation. "I don't have a lot to offer you, Carolyn. Can you be happy in Casey's Corners being a mother to the rug rats?"

She reached up and placed a hand on his cheek. "I can be happy wherever you are. You make me happy."

"Then you'll marry me? Help me keep my fairy tales straight?"

"Yes, yes, I'll marry you."

His lips descended to hers, seducing her with flames of passion, warming her with fires of love. When the kiss finally ended, they both turned toward the boys, who grinned at them from their snug cocoon amid the blankets.

"Ma-ma-ma." Trent bounced up and down on his plump little bottom.

"Da-da-da," Brent added, then giggled in delight.

Beau laughed and pulled Carolyn closer. "I think they knew all along we were going to be their parents."

Carolyn smiled up at him, knowing her happiness, her love shone from her eyes. "That's because they believe your fairy tales."

"What do you mean?"

"You don't always get the stories or the characters right, but you always manage to get to the proper ending."

His lips curved upward. "And that is?"

Carolyn snuggled against him and raised her lips toward his. "And they lived happily ever after," she murmured, as his lips claimed hers again.

Epilogue

"I told you so." Regina sat on the edge of the bed and grinned at Carolyn. "I knew you and Beau would get together."

"Oh, stop being so smug and help me with this veil." Carolyn's fingers trembled slightly as she carefully picked up the wedding veil attached to the small, beaded cap. As she positioned the cap on her head, Regina moved behind her to help with the lacy folds that cascaded down Carolyn's back.

When they were finished, Carolyn stepped in front of the dresser mirror and gazed at her reflection. A bride. Today she was a bride. It was still so hard to believe.

It had only been a week since Beau's proposal in the seedy motel room, but he had insisted on a wedding as soon as possible. They'd agreed on a home wedding, with the backyard serving as their chapel. From the curtained window Carolyn could hear the murmurs of the guests who awaited the beginning of the ceremony.

"Oh, honey, you look just beautiful." Regina's eyes filled with tears and she swiped at them with a small laugh. "Drat it, I always cry at weddings."

Carolyn leaned over and kissed her friend on the cheek. "Would you mind if I have a few minutes alone?"

"Of course not." Regina looked at her watch. "But just a moment or two. I think the whole town is here to see you and Beau get hitched." With another smile, Regina slipped out the bedroom door, leaving Carolyn alone with her thoughts.

She walked back over to the mirror, once again studying her reflection. This would be the last time she looked in a mirror and saw Carolyn Baker. After today, she would be Carolyn Randolf. Her heart swelled with happiness.

Reaching up with one hand, she grasped tightly the phoenix charm that hung around her neck. Her only regret was that neither her father nor Sam was here to give her away.

"Oh, Sam, I wish you were here." As she thought of her brother, her eyes burned hotly. How she wished he could walk her down the aisle. When would the mystery of Sam be solved? Carolyn knew all the pieces to her happiness would not be in place until Sam's disappearance was resolved.

"Carolyn?" Regina knocked softly on her door. "They're waiting for you."

After taking a deep breath and giving Carolyn Baker one final look in the mirror, she opened the bedroom door and joined Regina in the hall.

As they went through the house toward the back door, Carolyn heard the music begin to play, coming from the rented sound system. Regina gave Carolyn a hug, then turned and walked out the door and down the makeshift carpeted aisle between the rows of spectators.

As the stirring sounds of the "Wedding March" began, Carolyn stepped out the door, into the brilliant afternoon sunshine. People on either side of the aisle stood, all turning to look at her.

She walked slowly, self-consciously...until she saw Beau standing at the end of the aisle. He was clad in a tuxedo and babies. His smile, his eyes held the promise of a lifetime of love. As she continued, quickly now, Brent reached up and wrenched Beau's nose, and Trent yanked a strand of his tousled hair.

Laughing joyously, Carolyn increased her pace, hurrying toward her future, hurrying to her family.

*   *   *   *   *

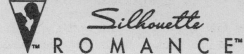

COMING NEXT MONTH

MILLION DOLLAR SWEEPSTAKES

Welcome to the

A new series
by Carol Grace

This bed and breakfast offers great views, gracious hospitality—and possibly even love!

You've already met proprietors Mandy and Adam Gray in LONELY MILLIONAIRE (Jan. '95). Now this happily married pair invite you to stay and share the romantic stories of how two other very special couples found love at the Miramar Inn:

ALMOST A HUSBAND—Carrie Stephens needed a fiancé—fast! And her partner, Matt Graham, was only too happy to accommodate, but could he let Carrie go when their charade ended?

AVAILABLE SEPTEMBER 1995

ALMOST MARRIED—Laurie Clayton was eager to baby-sit her precocious goddaughter—but she hadn't counted on Cooper Buckingham playing "daddy"!

AVAILABLE MARCH 1996

Don't miss these charming stories coming soon from

Silhouette ROMANCE™

Yo amo novelas con corazón!

Starting this March, Harlequin opens up to a whole new world of readers with two new romance lines in SPANISH!

Harlequin Deseo
- passionate, sensual and exciting stories

Harlequin Bianca
- romances that are fun, fresh and very contemporary

With four titles a month, each line will offer the same wonderfully romantic stories that you've come to love—now available in Spanish.

Look for them at selected retail outlets.

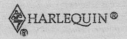 HARLEQUIN ®

As seen on TV!
Free Gift Offer

With a Free Gift proof-of-purchase from any Silhouette® book, you can receive a beautiful cubic zirconia pendant.

This gorgeous marquise-shaped stone is a genuine cubic zirconia—accented by an 18" gold tone necklace.

(Approximate retail value $19.95)

Send for yours today...
compliments of 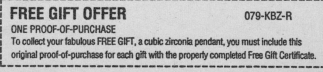 *Silhouette®*

To receive your free gift, a cubic zirconia pendant, send us one original proof-of-purchase, photocopies not accepted, from the back of any Silhouette Romance™, Silhouette Desire®, Silhouette Special Edition®, Silhouette Intimate Moments® or Silhouette Shadows™ title available in February, March or April at your favorite retail outlet, together with the Free Gift Certificate, plus a check or money order for $1.75 U.S./$2.25 CAN. (do not send cash) to cover postage and handling, payable to Silhouette Free Gift Offer. We will send you the specified gift. Allow 6 to 8 weeks for delivery. Offer good until April 30, 1996 or while quantities last. Offer valid in the U.S. and Canada only.

Free Gift Certificate

Name: _____

Address: _____

City: _____ State/Province: _____ Zip/Postal Code: _____

Mail this certificate, one proof-of-purchase and a check or money order for postage and handling to: SILHOUETTE FREE GIFT OFFER 1996. In the U.S.: 3010 Walden Avenue, P.O. Box 9057, Buffalo NY 14269-9057. In Canada: P.O. Box 622, Fort Erie,

---

FREE GIFT OFFER   079-KBZ-R

ONE PROOF-OF-PURCHASE

To collect your fabulous FREE GIFT, a cubic zirconia pendant, you must include this original proof-of-purchase for each gift with the property completed Free Gift Certificate.

079-KBZ-R